SAPLING

in the Brambles

SAPLING

in the Brambles

Will Erwin

Unlimited Publishing LLC

http://www.unlimitedpublishing.com

Copyright © 2010 by Will Erwin

First Edition

ISBN: 9781451585469

This fine book and many others are available at:
http://www.unlimitedpublishing.com

Unlimited Publishing LLC is a proud member of the Independent Book Publishers Association (IBPA-online.org), serving more than 3,000 publishers across North America and around the world.

P r o l o g u e

As Charlie Osgood closed the garage door behind his new pickup, he saw a car bearing the markings of Fairchild University slow down, then turn in the drive.

As his old, powerful and calloused hand opened the door into the house, he called, "Honey, they're here."

Annie Osgood put down her teapot, dried her hands, and straightened her white hair as she called back, "I'll get the door while you freshen up."

After the car stopped, a tall woman in a dark business suit emerged. She grabbed her briefcase from the back seat and looked around with interest as a younger woman in casual clothing followed her to the door.

"Mrs. Osgood?" The older woman spoke enthusiastically, a look of pride beaming from her green eyes.

"Yes." Annie Osgood adjusted her glasses to see them a little better.

"I'm Dr. Grace Cannon, and this is my associate Mary Palm. Thank you for agreeing to see us." She looked around admiringly. "This is a beautiful home. Quite new, isn't it?"

"Yes, we love it. It is so nice to have you join us."

Annie Osgood had an electric smile that made everyone else want to smile. She introduced her husband with obvious pride and gave the guests a quick tour of the house.

Once they were all comfortably seated, Dr. Cannon and Miss Palm set up tape recorders and took out notebooks. Dr. Cannon spoke. "As I mentioned in my letter, we are writing a history book, and you have information we need. We want to know about Joe Oberlin."

Charlie Osgood pulled up the footrest on his recliner as he asked, "What do you want to know about him? I met him before he was in the first grade, but Annie here knows more. Sisters always do."

"We would like to know about his life, his childhood, how he grew up, and as much as you can tell us about what happened to him in the war."

Annie's eyes sparkled. "Joe Oberlin was a big baby. He weighed ten and a half pounds at birth, and in the hospital, they called him Giant Joe. He not only was big, but also strong and fast — too fast.

"When he was two years old, he tore into the kitchen, stood up on his kiddie car, and flipped the handle on a pan of boiling milk. It came down all over him. His parents gave first aid to his face, but when they pulled his sweater off, the skin on his neck, shoulder, and arm came with it.

"Giant Joe became a puny, sick little fellow who was very shy. When he went swimming, everyone stared at the red, untanned, gnarly skin on his neck, shoulder, and arm. His parents said they stared because they cared, but he listened to the other kids who said, 'You're ugly.'

"When he entered the first grade, he had one ear infection after another, missing half the first grade. Joe became so deaf he couldn't hear a fire siren a block away.

In short, he was the worst athlete, the worst musician, and a near failure academically, due to time missed at school. Bear that in mind as you hear his story.

"Those years of the Great Depression and World War II were years of poverty, full living, opportunity, anguish, and death. It is not easy to explain."

BOOK I

Chapter I
1933
Humiliation and
the Great
Depression

The cold air nipped his nose, but Joe Oberlin stayed warm under his stack of old blankets. His mother called the top blanket a steamer rug. It was old and full of holes, but it held a lot of heat.

As he opened one eye and looked around, he recognized a hint of daylight coming. He heard footsteps as his father entered the bathroom next door, lifted the screen on the small, round kerosene heater, and lit the fire. Joe knew that his rest was near its end.

His father rose early every morning and lit the stove to warm the bathroom before he dressed so that Joe and then his mother and sister could follow in the warmth. He heard his father go down the stairs and then down another stairs to the basement. The grates banged loudly as his father shook the ashes out of the wood-burning furnace. He heard thumps as chunks of wood landed in the big old furnace. His father had opened the damper as he went down so that lots of air flowed through the furnace. The fire would roar by the time his mother came down and turned down the damper so the furnace wouldn't overheat.

Shortly, he heard, "Joe, up and at 'em. We have work to do."

Joe looked down at the steamer rug and saw the thin layer of snow drifted across it, as the late winter wind sneaked in through the cracks of their old wooden farmhouse. He gave his blanket a quick flip to throw the snow on the floor and felt the ice-cold boards under his feet. He ran as fast as he could to the bathroom. As he dressed, the smell of kerosene burned his nostrils, but the warmth felt good to his shivering body.

He came downstairs, reached in the wood box for kindling and some old newspaper, and started a fire in his mother's old wood range hoping that it would be warm enough to cook breakfast when Mother and his little sister arrived downstairs. Then he donned the soft cloth moccasins they wore to keep their feet from being too cold in their gum-rubber boots, as they did their chores. He slipped on his coveralls over his school clothes, put a heavy coat over the top, pulled a sock-cap down over his ears, and tied a scarf around his neck to keep the hay chaff and the small leaves of silage from coming down his neck. Then he went to the barn.

When he arrived at the barn, his father had already let the sheep out and was walking through to see how many ewes with newborns had stayed behind to be penned off. As he looked in the various small pens of ewes and lambs, he noticed that his dad had let out a couple of pairs of twins that had been born the day before and moved them into the west shed where they kept the stronger lambs and their mothers. The newborns now occupied these empty pens. He then looked at the third pen and saw the orphan lamb with the skin of the dead natural lamb tied on his back with binder twine. The mother was sniffing the hide of the dead lamb and permitting the adopted lamb to nurse. In the next pen, the family dog, a big gentle Collie, was sitting in the corner tied in the pen, not appreciating his job. He was doing it well because the mother was stomping her foot at the dog and permitting a previously rejected lamb to nurse because of her maternal instincts to defend from the dog.

He climbed up the silo, picked up the silage fork, and began throwing the ensilage down the chute, where he knew his father would shortly scoop it into baskets and carry it to the various feed bunks before he let the flock back in to eat. Joe never liked throwing the ensilage down the chute because it was like a chimney, and the light leaves were sucked back up and drifted down over his head, and if he wasn't careful, down his neck.

He forked silage until he heard the voice call up the chute, "That's enough. Come on down. We'll finish up and then go to breakfast."

They came in the backroom, pulled off their gumboots, peeled off their work coats and sock-caps, and hung them up. Joe also pulled off his coveralls and looked quickly over his school clothes to make sure there were no blemishes or spots of silage or something worse. Entering the kitchen was always a treat; something on the stove smelled good, and Mother was glad to see them.

The kitchen was austere. Plain, rough wooden chairs that needed paint surrounded a table covered with an old but spotlessly clean oil cloth. The floor was covered with linoleum which was worn through in spots. The giant kitchen stove dominated the room. A sink in the corner had iron streaks below the faucet. The plates were chipped, the water glasses an odd mixture, and the silverware showed spots of yellow where the plate had worn off, but all was immaculately clean. The room had an ambiance of warmth.

The great treat of the morning was the loud: "Hello, Papa. Hello, Joe," from his little sister, eight-year-old Annie, who had red hair, freckles on her nose, and a radiant smile. She was the perpetual enthusiast. "Do we have any new lambs today, Papa?"

"Yes, we had six — two pairs of twins and two singles, and they all seem to be healthy."

"How is the little orphan doing with the dead lamb's skin?"

"He's doing well. I think tomorrow we can take the skin off and, if the mother still owns him, we can turn him out."

"Oh, that's wonderful! Are we going to have any pets? I do hope I can have one to raise on a bottle."

"We probably will. It seems like we do every year, and they all love you."

In the background, Joe sang, "Annie had a little lamb, little lamb, little lamb." Annie gave him a friendly grin and continued to set the table.

Mother spoke cheerily, "I hope you like scrapple because that's all there is this morning." Scrapple was fundamentally a mixture of cornmeal and the chipped pork from their home-butchered hogs. They covered it with maple syrup — but not the best, first-run syrup. The first run sold for more money. Anything that would sell they had to sell. The family ate what was left. It was a filling breakfast, and shortly, it was time for the school bus.

Joe could never get on the school bus without his mother's inspection. She looked at him intently. "Come here, Joe, let me see you." She looked carefully at his face. "Did you scrub it hard?"

"Yes."

"Were you careful not to get barn smells on you?" His mother had a sense of smell like a vulture. People said that vultures found their food by their sense of smell, and his mother could find any smell that existed. She sniffed him. "You were careful about the ensilage. Have a good day at school."

Joe and Annie picked up their lunch boxes and books then went out the front door to wait for the bus.

As the children closed the door behind them, Mary Oberlin pushed a wisp of black hair from her forehead into the bun in back of her head. "Chris, how is Joe doing? I worry about him. Annie seems to have the world in her hand, but Joe has such a struggle."

Christopher Oberlin thought a minute. "Mary, he's a young man of good intention, but he is not very strong. I think he has to push himself to do his chores, but he doesn't complain. In the first grade, he was a leader for awhile until disaster struck, and he's been holding back ever since."

Mary's hazel eyes were penetrating. "That was so embarrassing."

"It shouldn't have been. It was a case of a smart, good kid getting a bad break."

"It showed poor home training."

"I don't think so." Chris was blunt as his large calloused hands put his coffee cup firmly on the table.

Mary looked at him with wide eyes. "Why?"

"Remember when Ed and I went to school and checked things out. We were sure he got a bum rap."

Their cousin Ed had always shared an interest in Joe, but Mary didn't know about their visit to the school. "How so?"

"As a farm boy, he had helped me drain ponds, and at the county fair, he saw the urinals were sloping, tin troughs that drained down to the sewer."

"What does that have to do with it?"

"Those urinals at school go clear to the floor and the concrete floor slopes to the urinal. Furthermore, when you flush the urinal, it sprays out and washes down the sloping concrete." Chris took the last bit of his scrapple and continued. "The first graders hated them because it was hard to reach up and flush, and the water sprayed over their feet. To six year olds, standing in line to use a urinal during recess was a waste of valuable time. Joe's idea to stand in small circles and use the sloping floor cut the time by one-third and reduced the risk of getting sprayed when you flushed to one in three or four. Since the spray washed the floor anyway, he figured it was sanitary." Chris got up and put his dish in the sink.

Mary picked up her own plate and carried it to the counter. "Why did it go so badly?"

"It didn't at first. The other little boys thought he was a brilliant leader."

Getting a little impatient with her husband's drawn-out tale, Mary asked again, "Why did it turn out so badly?"

"Chet Barnes is a very conscientious janitor, and when he happened in a few days later and saw what was going on, he

exploded in a rage and terrified the kids. They all blamed Joe."
Chris turned to grab his heavy coat off a wall peg.

Mary followed him to the door. "Didn't anyone explain it to the janitor?"

"Ed and I tried. We even showed him the slope and the spray. He backed off some. I think he understood and felt a little sorry for Joe, but he said he couldn't do much or people would call him a janitor who approved of urinating on the floor. Joe was the scapegoat."

Mary shook her head. "Poor, dear little Joe. That was years ago. Do you think it will permanently damage ingenuity and destroy any leadership ability?"

Chris scratched his head. "No, we all take a tumble now and then. I think his burns hurt him more. They're ugly and they've made him puny. His Uncle Ed says, 'Don't worry; the kid will be all right. He'll grow out of all these troubles. He has what it takes. He's a winner.'"

Mary was sad. "It's so hard to see, now, and it's so hard on him. He told me when the boys choose ball teams they choose him last, and if the number comes out odd, they argue over which team has to take him because nobody wants him. That's a lot for a twelve year old to bear."

"Ed says it will make him tough and toughness counts in life; Ed ought to know, he's been through a lot."

Mary thought a minute. "Yes, he's been through a lot, but he's given a lot, and he was lucky enough to end up married to Eve."

Chris grinned. "Yeah, he sure was. But as to Joe, all we can do is teach him good habits, good values, let him know how much we love him, and thank God for the support that Eve and Ed give him. The four of us can do a lot for a good kid who's had a bunch of tough breaks."

#

When the bus arrived at school, Annie ran off to meet her waiting friends, all of whom relished the sight of her. They surrounded her, as they happily made their way toward the second grade room. Joe walked off the bus alone and quietly walked up the steps toward the sixth grade saying hi to a few classmates and went into his room.

As he entered the room, Miss Hendricks, an older, fierce-looking teacher who created much awe among her students, gave him a warm smile. "Good morning, Joe."

He said good morning and smiled back. As he walked toward his desk, he heard Sam Dugan say in a soft voice, "Teacher's pet."

Joe said nothing but thought that if he did get a good response from the teacher it was because he tried hard, while Sam was more interested in cutting up. He felt some twinge of anxiety because he knew that he would take some rough stuff on the playground because of Sam and his friends' attitude toward any teacher's pet.

#

When Chris Oberlin came in for lunch, the big, six-foot, heavy-boned, powerful ex-tackle sat down in the wooden chair opposite Mary. As Mary finished blessing their lunch, his brown eyes were sad. "I've been thinking about Joe most of the morning. It tears me up. He's a good-hearted kid and he tries hard, but I'm worried about his confidence. He carries such a load inside — take his first grade problem. The other kids have forgotten. Chet, the janitor, understands and really likes Joe, but Joe carries it like he does his burn scars and it holds him back. The teachers say he does well when he's confident and not well when he's not. When he's out playing with the kids, he always seems to be the loser."

Mary looked out the window at the open fields of winter. "I'm worried about Joe, too. So is Eve. She won't admit it; she always says good things about everybody or says nothing. I really think with Eve, if you talked about John Dillinger, she would find something good about him, but I can tell underneath the skin that she's worried. It's interesting; all three of us seem to be more worried than Ed.

"Ed says Joe is an awfully good shot. Give him some ammunition, explain to him how hard up we all are, and see if he can bring in some rabbits the first time we have a big snow. They're easy to track. Make it tough for him, but give him a chance to be a winner."

"I'll do that, but I'm afraid it's going to take more than that, Mary. He loves the farm. I don't know how I'm going to get the courage to tell him that we can't make the next payment on the mortgage and we will probably lose it."

Mary's face was drawn. She was naturally trim but strong. There was no sparkle to her hazel eyes as she spoke. "That will be hard on him. I don't think he senses the degree to which we're hurting. Joe is better dressed than most of the kids in his class thanks to the family hand-me-downs that came from family in Chicago. We eat pretty well off the farm, so Joe hasn't felt the pressure. There is some talk about the Federal Land Bank being more lenient, but it is a faint hope."

Chris's appetite slackened as he spoke. "I'll hold off a little while and try to ease him into it. In the meantime, I'm going to let him go out on his own with the single shot 22 and see if he can bring in some rabbits. If he has really good luck, it will be a big plus for him and a good thing for us." Then a flicker of a smile went across his face. "At least we don't have to worry about Annie. If we were dead broke and had to live in an igloo, she would say, 'Isn't the ice on the walls beautiful?'"

Mary laughed. "We are blessed."

#

That Friday night one of those beautiful snowfalls where the snow comes slowly in large flakes descended on the farm. Early Saturday morning, Joe listened as his father spoke. "You're going hunting today. We are hard up and we need all the food we can get. There are brush piles on the back forty where we cleaned up the fencerow. The rabbits nest in them and then move out into the corn stubble to feed. It ought to be easy to track them.

"You should be able to shoot them in the head, and if you have to, your Uncle Ed says you can even hit them on the run because you know how to lead them. I'm giving you the 22 and I'm giving you fifteen shells. When you come back, I want something to eat for each shell. So take your time, don't be in a hurry; only take good shots because we can't afford more ammunition. Above all, be careful. Remember the gun is always loaded. Never point it at yourself or anybody else. Don't cock it until you're ready to fire and make sure it's not cocked any time you're carrying it."

Joe looked solemn. "Dad, I'm not sure I can hit every time."

"Make sure, Joe. Your Uncle Ed says you're a crackin' good shot, so take your time, don't waste the ammo, and do your best. If you miss one, I'm not going to have a fit, but don't miss a lot."

Joe wiggled his nose and grinned at his father. "You're a pretty tough old buzzard."

Chris warmed inside, as he knew this was real affection.

#

Joe walked through the snow and watched the large snowflakes gently sifting down onto the barely frozen ground. The trees looked like a picture from a Christmas card. He looked at the rising sun and thought what a marvelous experience it is to live on this earth and what a joy it is to have such a wonderful farm.

He approached the back forty, saw faint movements around the brush piles, and walked slowly. In the cornfield, he saw tracks where the rabbits hopped along and stopped to feed. Very shortly, he saw a huge healthy rabbit take a couple of bites and hop on, then hold very still as he heard noise. Joe raised his rifle, fired, hit the rabbit in the head, and ran up to decapitate it, so it would bleed well. He stuck it in the gunnysack he had tied to his belt. At another brush pile, he quietly waited to see if others would come out. The same thing happened until he had six rabbits, the most anybody had brought in for a long time; and they were all big. However, the rabbits were getting a little more shy and wary. He waited awhile and was able to get one more. Joe decided they were scared out, but seven big fat rabbits was a lot of meat.

As he started toward the house, not knowing what he would see, he reloaded his rifle hoping for one last chance. When he neared the edge of the cornfield, a rabbit, which had apparently been running in the corn stubble ahead of him, jumped into the open and ran to the right. He cocked the rifle, led the rabbit, estimated how much it would bounce up, and fired hitting the rabbit in the chest rolling it end over end. He added it to his bag. He'd never really hit a rabbit on the run before. He was going back to see his father, eight for eight. Granted seven of them he shot sitting when any idiot couldn't miss, but he'd gotten one on the run. He felt a mixture of success and pain. He didn't like killing, but he knew people had to eat.

As he walked toward the house with his bag of rabbits over his shoulder, (the bag having long since become too heavy for his belt) he anticipated his parent's response with relish.

At the back door, he called, "Mom, I got some rabbits."

His mother came out, looked at the size of the bag, and immediately gave a clang to the dinner bell, which meant: *Dad, come, I need you for something.* As they opened the bag and laid out the eight large plump rabbits, his father came around the corner, saw the rabbits, and grinned. Joe walked up to his father and handed him the rifle and seven unused cartridges. He looked at him with affection. "You're a pretty stingy old buzzard, but I made it by your rules."

As Mary, Chris, and Joe Oberlin were skinning and cutting up rabbit meat, Chris grinned. "You took my advice and shot them sitting, didn't you?"

Joe remained silent.

Suddenly there was an exclamation. "Joe, this one is shot through the chest! I thought I told you to shoot through the head."

Joe looked down. "I shot him on the run, Dad."

His father showed instant appreciation. "Good for you, Joe. That's really something. You shot him on the run with a 22. That's great." Joe tried not to change expression but felt larger in the chest.

His mother's eyes sparkled. "This is wonderful. We'll take rabbit stew to the potluck tomorrow. We'll have to take at least one to Uncle Ed and Aunt Eve, and I think we should take one to Mrs. Osgood. That amazing woman is a single mother raising four kids on the fifteen cents an hour she earns working in the telephone office. Furthermore, they're marvelous people, and meat will be a treat for them." They all silently agreed with Mary's decision.

Sunday night at the church potluck, all four of the Osgood kids made it a point to thank Joe for the rabbit and tell him how good it was.

Joe thought the Osgood kids were good. They had good manners and were honest. It was fun to have them as friends. Mrs. Osgood not only thanked him but also gave him a big hug.

As they were waiting for dinner to start at the church, Joe was chatting with the Osgoods when he noticed a rather animated conversation among the men. He heard one say in a rather loud voice, "No kidding," and noticed three or four heads turn to look at him. It really didn't cross his mind what might be going on, he just felt embarrassed. Ever since his burns, when he would go swimming and everybody would stare at the swirled skin in the large, raw, red areas over his neck, shoulder, and arm, he felt embarrassment when people looked at him. He wanted to withdraw but looked away and said nothing.

When they lined up for dinner, Sam Johnson, the young, popular undertaker, slapped him gently on the shoulder and grinned. "Nice going — eight for eight."

Joe felt goose bumps. He was getting approval from outside his family.

They drove home, the six of them, Chris and Mary, Annie and Joe, Aunt Eve and Uncle Ed, whom they always picked up whenever they could so that they could ride together. Uncle Ed smiled warmly. "Joe, I'm proud of you for the one you got on the run because you had to calculate lead two ways, once for the rabbit's speed and once for his up and down bounce. That's good shooting."

Joe answered with a new-found confidence. "Thanks, Uncle Ed, but isn't it bad manners for a teacher to brag on his student?"

Uncle Ed chuckled, but outright laughter came out of Aunt Eve, Annie, and his parents.

#

That evening, as they walked in the house, Mary whispered softly to Chris, "He's feeling pretty good about himself now; if you need to tell him about the problems with the farm, this might be a good time."

As they finished the family game of dominoes, Mary rose and said to Annie, "I need you to help me in the kitchen," and then looked at Chris and smiled.

When the ladies had left, Chris looked over at Joe. "Joe, you're growing up and I need to talk to you about some of the things that are a part of life that you need to know about."

"What do you mean, Dad?"

"Joe, this Depression is very serious. We borrowed a lot of money to make our farm bigger before prices went down, and we owe the bank a lot of money on our crops and livestock. We also owe the insurance company a lot of money on the farm. If we sell all of our crops and livestock, we can pay off the bank, but we don't have enough money to make our payment to the insurance company that holds the mortgage on the land. There's a very good chance, a probability in fact, that they will take our farm away from us this year."

Joe looked at him. "You mean take everything? We won't have anything? We won't have a house, we won't have animals, and we won't have our land or woods?"

"Yes. There's some talk that the Federal Land Bank might be more lenient, but if we can't find a way out, we'll lose everything. When you look at the prices and figure out what our land is worth, what we owe is greater than the value of everything we have."

Joe was stunned. He felt kind of sick as he asked, "What about Uncle Ed and Aunt Eve? They have more money than we do. Can't they help us?"

"Joe, in life we have to do things on our own; we don't expect our family to help us. Uncle Ed and Aunt Eve are all we could ask for, both as family and as friends, but not only could I not ask them, I couldn't let them if they offered. Because, Joe, another thing that you're going to have to face is that sometimes not everyone has good health. Sometimes it takes a lot of money and a lot of time. Sometimes people even die. If you haven't noticed, Aunt Eve is not feeling well, and we could never let them give us money if it would interfere with Aunt Eve getting the best possible care when she's sick."

Joe immediately forgot about the farm. "Oh, of course not. We want to do everything for Aunt Eve. Is she bad sick, Dad? I know she hasn't been feeling well, but I thought it was just the flu or something."

His father looked gloomy. "I hate to talk with you about it because Aunt Eve doesn't want anybody to know, but it could be very serious. They've gone to a couple of specialists who told them that in all probability she has an abdominal cancer and this could very well, in a few years, take her life. She doesn't want to talk about it, so we won't talk about it."

Joe looked at his father. "I thought losing the farm would be the worst thing that could ever happen to us, but it isn't. The worst thing that could ever happen would be to lose you, or Mom, or Annie, or Uncle Ed, or Aunt Eve. Maybe we'll have to lose both."

Chris stood up, walked over, and put his hand on Joe's shoulder. "Son, I hate to put so much on you so fast, but you're a strong young man. When you say your prayers tonight, just add one for Aunt Eve and add one for our family and the farm. Remember, no matter how tough things get, we can lighten that burden by giving to others in every way we can. When you go to sleep tonight, I want you to think about the people at the church enjoying their rabbit stew and about how happy the Osgoods were to have the good rabbit meat."

Joe smiled faintly. "Thanks, Dad. Good night."

A few days later, as Joe and his dad were walking to the backfield to bring up some yearling heifers to the barn, Joe was thoughtful. "Dad, since we talked man to man, there's something I want to know."

His father was amused. "What is it, Joe?"

"I want to know about Uncle Ed and Aunt Eve 'cause I understand Aunt Eve really isn't my aunt, she's your cousin."

"That's right. She was a couple of years ahead of me in school, and she was great."

"How was she great?"

"She wasn't a pretty girl, but she was so beautiful we all loved her."

"Dad, you are confusing me. How could she be beautiful if she wasn't pretty?"

"She always thought about the other person. Even when she was in competition and lost she would be so happy for the winner that she didn't have time to think about losing. In her spare time, she was always finding nice things to do for people. She would knit heavy socks for me to wear in the winter. I have never known anyone like her. She brings out the best in all of us."

Joe cocked his head and mulled it over a bit. "I understand that Uncle Ed doesn't talk much about his past. He's been my Sunday school teacher for three years now. He is very much against anybody drinking alcohol, but I don't know anything about what happened to him before he came to Indiana."

"I figured that question would come up some day. I don't know it all. I can tell you some of it, but there is a lot I don't know about. Ed, even though he is the husband of my cousin, is an uncle in every way to you, and a brother to me. He doesn't say much about his past.

"He was a pilot in France in the war. I have heard that he was a very good pilot. He shot down some German airplanes, and he drank too much. I don't know much about what happened there and Ed doesn't talk about it. However, I know that after the war, his drinking got the best of him, and he became an alcoholic. A truck smashed into him injuring him badly; that's why he walks with a limp. He does the shop work and I do the field work because he can't walk behind the horses. When he was injured so badly and in the hospital, he met Aunt Eve, who was a nurse there."

Joe looked up at the popcorn clouds in the sky and thought about Uncle Ed flying and what an awful comedown it must have been to be an alcoholic and then be all smashed up. His eyes grew moist as he listened.

"You know Aunt Eve: anybody who was in the hospital and being taken care of by Aunt Eve would think he'd been around an angel. While he was so sick, Aunt Eve was attentive and kind; she showed him a kind of love he'd never seen. I don't mean a woman for a man love; I mean love in the sense like the church teaches. That's when he realized there had to be a greater force than he knew. When the chaplains came to the hospital to talk to him, he listened. He recognized that faith could be the answer to what drove him to drinking. I think he decided that he really couldn't live without marrying Eve because apparently it all fell together at once, his love for Eve, his ability to stop drinking, and his depth of Christian commitment. At any rate, you have a great Sunday school teacher and a great uncle out of it. When they wrote us asked if we knew where there was a farm for sale, we were happy to write back about the farm next to us."

"I wonder what he did in France. You think he really shot down enemy airplanes? Did he shoot down several?"

The heifers started to spread out. Without any instruction, Joe moved farther from his father to keep them walking next to the fence. When the heifers bunched and were walking gently, he moved closer to his father who raised his voice slightly.

"Joe, I think so. I can't prove it because he never told me. I only read it between the lines in a comment that Aunt Eve made, and she won't talk about it either because Ed doesn't want to talk about it. I recommend that you never ask him. It may come some time, but I wouldn't ask. I think it's the pain of having lost so many friends. Maybe it was hard on him to realize that he was shooting at other human beings. Whatever it is, it's so painful he doesn't want to talk about it."

"I can understand that. It would be horrible to have to kill another human being even in a war."

"Ed could do it, Joe. He's strong. If he didn't get the enemy, the enemy would kill his friends or him. I think that's why the army is so tough about discipline and drill. They want you to do what you have to do without thinking about it."

"Okay, Dad, but what about Aunt Eve? Is she any better? Do we know anything about her?"

"No, son, there are some things in life that we don't know until they happen. Lots of things are that way."

The heifers moved gently through the open gate of the barnyard. Joe looked at his big and powerful father and saw gentleness. The heifers felt it, too. The drive had been as easy as the conversation was hard.

Chapter II
1935
The Challenge and Death

Ed Riley was sandy-haired, blue-eyed, quick moving and agile despite his injured leg. He had a habit of flipping his head to get his hair back before he started a task. He flipped his hair now, as he spoke. "Joe, you're fifteen now and your dad says you can work part-time with me, and I have an idea. I want to make a partnership with you."

Joe's spirits rose. "What are we going to do, Uncle Ed?"

"Been watching down at the sale barn. Livestock is selling cheap. Nobody has much money to buy anything. When they bring in animals with bad feet, bad eyes, abscesses or other things wrong with them, they sell for almost nothing. Sometimes, they sell for a good bit less than the hides would bring if we skinned them out.

"I have this bad leg; I can't get around much, but I can work on animals. I've been reading books on animal health and talked to the veterinarian some. We can't afford to pay veterinarians, but a lot of treatment is just a matter of taking care of them. If they sell cheaper than the hides, if they die, we can skin them and sell the hides. If they live, they may be worth something. These terrible low prices can't stay this low. If we can hold on, we might make a good bit of money, but we wouldn't have to put much money out. We'd have to put in doctoring time for me and chasing time for you. I'll put up the money and charge interest; you do the chasing and help me with the doctoring. I'll furnish the grass 'cause it won't take much for a while, and if we get a lot, then we'll pay rent to me for the grass or whatever we have to use. If we make money, you're my partner and you'll get half. If we don't make money, all you've lost is your time. I'll have the fun of having a partner and a chance to make some money, and you'll get a chance to bet not getting wages against making pretty good money. You want the deal or not?"

"I'd like to say yes, but I want to talk to my dad first."

Ed grinned. "You're going to make a business man, Joe. A wise man always talks it over with somebody he trusts before he jumps into something."

"It isn't that I don't trust you, Uncle Ed. I trust you with everything. I just like to have my dad in the loop in everything I do."

"I understand. I didn't think you didn't trust me. You just know when a man has good judgment and you're smart enough to want to share in it."

"That's right. Thanks. Do you care if I go home and talk to Dad right now?"

"Run ahead, Joe."

Joe came tearing in the driveway, went straight to the barn, ran up to his dad, and poured out the whole offer Uncle Ed had given to him not realizing that Uncle Ed had received his father's approval long before it was ever mentioned to Joe.

Chris Oberlin was thoughtful. "When you go into a partnership with somebody, you have to have complete trust in the other person. You can completely trust your Uncle Ed. You also need to think of what you're going to lose, and all you're going to lose is your time. What are you going to make? You might make a little money, and if things turn around, you might make a good bit of money. Since the Federal Land Bank took our mortgage, we have a little wiggle room financially. You help me with half your spare time and put half with Ed. It will only take a lot of time on sale days when you drive them back from the sale barn. On the other days, you can do it in an hour or so. I think it's a great idea. If I were you, I'd do it."

"I will." Joe turned and ran back down the driveway.

He ran a few steps, stopped in his tracks, turned around, and ran back. "Dad, I just thought . . . do I have enough to give to be a fair deal to Uncle Ed?"

"I'm proud of you for thinking of that, Joe. Yes, I think you do. Ed doesn't get around very well. He can't chase the animals and you can. He says you are a young man with a great future. Ed is a man who looks ahead, and he's betting on not only what you are now but what you're going to be. I think you have enough to give a fair share in this partnership."

"Thanks, Dad." Joe wheeled and ran.

The next sale day, Joe could hardly wait until school was out. He ran to the sale barn, up into the bleachers, and sat down beside Uncle Ed.

"What do we have so far?"

"Twenty of the skinniest hogs you ever saw. They came from Clem Boggs' farm. You know Clem doesn't feed them. He just lets them go out in the corn, eat, and inbreed badly until they get so overpopulated he has to get rid of some of them. We have ten sows and ten gilts that look like Razorbacks; nobody wanted them. We're going to see if we can worm them here at the sale barn before we leave. We also have some sheep. Dogs tore the ears up and made big gashes in the sides of the ewes. The guy who owned them didn't want to doctor them, so he brought them in here for what they'd bring. We have several odds and ends of cattle — most just abscesses and bad feet. They're just now bringing in a horse that I think we want to take a long look at." Joe turned and looked as a giant Shire gelding came through the door walking on three feet.

"Joe, I looked at him out in the back of the barn. I think something has run into his foot and he has a bad infection. I was able to touch it and it feels hot. It feels pretty firm. I suspect his owners couldn't find anything or were unable to dig it out if they did. It's not draining. He's awfully skinny and looks bad, but if we could cure that foot, what a whale of a horse he would be. I think he would weigh a ton. If we can't cure it, the hide will bring a good bit."

As the giant horse hobbled across the arena, Joe looked at him intently. "He's the biggest horse I ever saw, and he has a kindly face even when he's hurting."

"I noticed that, too."

No one bid on the horse. Finally, Ed called out, "Two dollars." Somebody else bid three. Ed bid, "Four dollars." No one else bid. Ed whispered, "The hide would bring five."

Joe frowned. "I want to save that horse."

After the sale, Joe arranged to meet one of the Osgood boys, and they drove their motley herd of beasts to the farm where Ed was waiting with needle and thread, hot water, antiseptic, knife, and some probing equipment. They were able to sew the loose ears back onto the sheep, sew up the worst of the gashes, and disinfect the cuts. They lanced the abscesses on the cattle, disinfected them, and treated their feet by pouring hot water with copper sulfate into a footbath and walking the sore-footed cattle through it.

Joe sensed something more than business. Uncle Ed liked animals. What they were doing was good even if it didn't make money. He would learn all he could to be a good partner. He couldn't make a team at school, but he was going to make this team work. He was proud to be part of a good thing.

Next came the giant horse. They took a huge hay rope down from the haymow and prepared a crowed gate under some strong beams where they could tie the horse and lift his infected foot. As they tied the horse, they had no difficulty. He was a gentle beast, but his power was so great they had some fear knowing that any animal under pain would strike out. When they had the giant gelding firmly secured, they put another rope around the infected foot, threw it over a beam, and pulled it up to hold it as firmly as possible. Uncle Ed then gently took his hoof-pruning knife and pealed away the dirt and loose chips around the center of the hoof. It was clear that it had been examined before and nothing had been found. However, in the center area, there was a slit with nothing showing. Having anticipated the problem, Ed reached in his pocket and pulled out a long, narrow nail, which he pushed into the slit. "There it is."

"What is it?"

"It's something hard. I suspect a piece of steel. It's been pushed on in and you can't see it from the surface; it's almost a half an inch before you hit it. Now we'll have to see if we can get it out."

He took a pair of long-nosed pliers, pushed them into the slit, and grasped several times on the foreign object, each time slipping off. The giant horse flinched and tensed his muscles, but he didn't try to break loose. As he slipped off, Ed rotated the pliers until he found an unusually firm grip, grabbed both hands on the handles of the pliers, pulled very hard, and it began to move. The pressure from the infection and the lubrication of the puss made it come very rapidly. A long, narrow piece of steel came from the hoof. Puss gushed out behind it. Ed yelled, "Bingo!"

Joe gasped, "You just named him!"

Ed then went over to his cabinet and pulled out a trocar and cannula, an instrument used for letting the gas out of the stomachs of bloated animals. It was a narrow, very sharp, nail-like thing, covered with a hollow tube so that when you poked it into the animal's side, pulled out the pointed piece of steel, the narrow tube stayed in and let the gas escape and the animal live. Ed carefully measured how far it was from the bottom of the hoof to where the steel had been. Then he took a hacksaw and cut off the hollow tube to be the same length. He put the tube on the pointed spike and inserted it into where he had removed the steel, pulled out the pin, and left the tube.

"Why did you do that?"

"I was afraid the pressure on the hoof wouldn't let it drain, and we need to keep the hole open. We'll watch it very closely and keep it open until there's no longer any ooze, and then we'll pull it out. Right now we need to get some warm water and hot rags and wrap that infected foot."

As Joe wrapped the rags soaked in hot water around the foot of the now released giant gelding, he felt Bingo's upper lip reach down and nuzzle his back with appreciation. Apparently, the warm water felt good, and this gentle beast was a people liker. The idea of saving this animal and working with him thrilled Joe.

#

A couple of months later, Mary Oberlin and Eve were crocheting rugs. They had cut old clothes into strips and were using oversized crochet hooks to make circles that eventually grew into an oval or circular rug. They weren't fancy rugs, but they cost nothing, and they kept bare feet off cold floors.

Mary needed to talk. "I'm worried, Eve."

"What about?"

"Joe."

Eve put down her crochet hook and with concern asked, "Why?"

"Chris told me that he went into the barn last evening and heard sobbing up in the haymow. He climbed up the ladder and found Joe behind a pile of hay up by the edge of the roof crying."

"Oh, dear."

"Joe was embarrassed and quickly went to work, but Chris checked the spot and said the hay was tramped down. He thinks that was Joe's secret retreat."

Worry clouded Eve's face." You mean he had been doing this a lot?"

"Chris thinks so. None of us has seen him cry for years. Maybe it's a good thing he has a secret place to let it all out. Some of the kids at school are just plain cruel."

"It's strange, Mary, friends talk to me about what a great kid he is."

"How so?"

"It used to be about how polite, thoughtful, and sincere he was, but lately, it's been about Bingo."

"Bingo?"

"Yes. They see that frail young man riding that huge horse with no saddle and often no bridle and they can't believe their eyes. Some say it looks like something out of a fairytale or a Greek myth."

"You know, Eve, it's a real friendship. When Bingo sees Joe he nickers and runs to the gate. Joe lets him out and Bingo follows him like a dog. Bingo is so tall that Joe can't get on his back from the ground, so he climbs up on a fence and tells Bingo to come. Then he climbs on. He rides bareback. When he doesn't have a bridle, he guides him with his knees."

"How did all this happen?"

"It started when Joe was hot packing his infected hoof. Then Joe started taking him treats. At school after lunch, when the other boys play ball and do macho things, Joe goes around gathering up the apple cores for Bingo. Bingo loves apple cores and lumps of sugar, but it's more than that — they really like each other."

"It sounds like they're best friends."

"Oh dear, Eve, don't say that. Annie heard someone say that at school and she came home devastated insisting that she was Joe's best friend. The only way I could console her was to get Joe to explain that Bingo was his best friend outside the family."

"Mary, it's strange. Our generation grew up with horses and is awed by Joe's horse skills, but his schoolmates are car crazy and think he's silly."

"The schoolmates are wrong. Joe learns from Bingo. He senses his fears, feels his moods, and knows when to reassure him. He's developing instincts and an ability to read silent communication that will help him all his life. Furthermore, he cares for Bingo and Bingo cares back; a car can't do that.

"Did you hear what happened at Smith's potato farm? Joe knew many of the kids from school were picking up potatoes behind the digger last Saturday, so he rode Bingo over to see what was going on. He was afraid the tractor and potato digger might frighten Bingo, so he tied Bingo to the fence and walked over to talk to the Osgood kids. Some bullies from school knew that frightened horses always run home, so they untied Bingo, hit him with sticks, and yelled at him. Bingo started to run home, but Joe yelled to Bingo and the giant horse turned completely around and ran to Joe. The Osgood kids boosted Joe up on to Bingo and those bullies hurried out of the way when Joe and Bingo came in their direction."

"Oh, Mary, that's wonderful. Joe needed that."

#

A few weeks later, Uncle Ed was taking Aunt Eve to a specialist. Since it was a school holiday, he told Joe to do the buying.

Joe was pleased, scared, and excited about the challenge. During the auction, he bought the usual infected and injured animals at the usual price, but toward the end of the sale, they drove in twenty goats. There was much hilarity, much laughing, and nobody wanted to buy the goats. Nobody, even in the Depression, wanted to eat goat meat. He didn't know whether goat hides would sell for anything, and goats were notorious for getting out and eating everything in sight, smelling bad, and giving people lots of problems. Nobody would bid.

Finally, the auctioneer begged, "Will anybody give a bid on the lot?"

Joe bid, "One dollar."

The auctioneer cried the sale a little longer, and then gave up. "Sold, for one dollar."

Joe was worried. Uncle Ed had never mentioned goats; he hadn't authorized goats. He didn't know what the hides would bring, but he figured that he could surely get a dollar for that many goat hides. He also had another idea of what those goats could do.

The next day, Uncle Ed congratulated him on the animals he'd purchased and was pleased with Joe's efforts in draining abscesses and sewing up wounds. However, he could see that Joe had something else on his mind. "What is it, Joe?"

"Come with me to the other side of the barn." Ed followed him and looked at a large pen to see twenty goats that had obviously already eaten the bedding straw that Joe had spread on the floor and were chewing on various wooden objects.

"What's this, Joe?"

"Nobody wanted them and they cost a dollar."

"It will be a lot of work for you, Joe, but we can surely get a dollar for that many goat skins."

"I have another idea."

"What's that, Joe?"

"You have a lot of weeds, briars, and brush growing up in the corners of some of your fields. It would take a lot of chopping and grubbing to clean them out. You have a couple rolls of picket fence out by the barn. I was wondering if we couldn't take these goats, who they say will eat anything, fence off those spots that are growing up to brush, and let the goats clean them up."

Ed was thoughtful. "Joe, you can think; you think of what other people may not have thought about. I think that's a good idea. Furthermore, you know how to cover your back trail. If it doesn't work, we can surely get a buck for the hides. As soon as we can drive the stakes in the ground, we're going to try that; it sure does beat taking a grub hoe and an axe and cleaning those places up."

One evening Chris Oberlin showed Joe a story in the paper about a man who boiled up the meat from his dead animals and fed it to his hogs. "I suggest that you chat with Ed. If he could make a furnace and a water tank where you could boil up the dead meat, I would furnish the wood for the fire in exchange for cooked meat as a protein for my hogs. You would have protein for your partnership hogs, and it would get you out of a lot of work burying carcasses. Within a week, Ed had produced a meat cooker and they were in business.

Things at school went pretty much the same for Joe except that the jokesters and the hecklers called him bloody Joe, the carcass kid, skinner, and the sick-critter getter. Joe didn't like it much, but time spent with the animals beat the ridicule that landed on him when he tried to play ball.

One evening, Joe sought out his dad. "Can we talk?"

"Sure." Chris scooted over on the swing to give Joe room to sit down.

Joe slumped back in the seat. "Were things hard for you in school when you were a kid?"

"Some, everybody has hard times. Why do you ask?"

"'Cause I hurt."

"Why?"

Joe shrugged as he felt his father's concern. "The town kids call the country kids hicks."

Chris laughed and sat back, rocking the swing. "That's not new. Anyway, it wears off as you get older."

Joe sighed, looking up at the full moon as it rose over the fields. "That's not the real problem."

The swing squeaked as Chris asked, "What is?"

"Me."

"Why?"

"I'm a bust."

"How?"

"I'm dumb."

"No you aren't. You missed half the first grade with ear infections, but your grades have been better every year since."

"You know what my teacher said?"

"Tell me."

"She is a friend of Annie's teacher. She said to me, 'We don't expect you to be as good as Annie, but we expect you to be better than you are.'"

"Joe, you know I won't lie to you. You are just as smart as Annie. Annie didn't miss half the first grade."

"But, Dad, I'm a flop."

"We all think that about ourselves from time to time."

"But I really am a bust."

"Why do you think so?"

"I can't even recognize most tunes."

"Neither could General Grant."

"Really?"

"Yes."

"I'm still a bust. I'm smaller, slower, and weaker than the other kids."

"You'll outgrow it. It takes time to get over bad burns."

"But it's so humiliating."

"How?"

"You know Sarah Hughes and how cute she is? Last week she fell down on the playground and I went over to help her up. She put out her hand and I took it and pulled, but she didn't come up. I fell down!"

Joe's eyes blinked in moisture. "Everybody on the playground laughed and hooted."

"Just hang in there, Joe. Uncle Ed and I are both sure that you'll be one of the biggest and strongest before long."

"Maybe, but I have to live today and I'm a failure. My grades aren't that good. I'm the worst athlete in school. I mess up in music, and the kids don't like me much 'cause I can't do anything well."

"You can shoot."

"Who cares?"

"You're a partner in a business."

"My uncle did that for me."

"You earned it."

"That isn't proven yet."

"You're honest."

"So what?"

"Weren't you one of only five kids in the whole school who the principal secretly asked to carry marked money so they could catch a thief?"

"Yes."

"That means that those who really know think you are one of the very best."

"Thanks, Dad, but I still have to live with the other kids and they don't think much of me."

"Uncle Ed thinks that's a good thing. He says it will make you strong, so when others fall into the kind of pit that he fell into you won't."

"Do you think he's right?"

"Yes, I'm sure of it. I wouldn't trade you for a carload of singers and all the athletes in school."

Joe grinned. "You are a biased old buzzard but hang onto the bias."

#

As the months went by, the herds of healthy animals began to grow. They had a good-looking herd of cattle, a nice flock of sheep, a bunch of hogs, an ever-expanding herd of brush-grubbing goats, and three healthy horses. However, as their livestock herds grew in health and numbers, Aunt Eve seemed to get weaker and weaker. Uncle Ed spent more time with her and more time going to doctors. Joe's dad spent more time helping the partnership while his mom and sister Annie spent more time with Aunt Eve. It seemed to Joe that Aunt Eve was a little weaker physically but maybe stronger in spirit. She never complained about anything, was always interested in everyone else, and found nothing but good in everybody she saw and anybody anyone talked about, particularly if someone was saying something bad. Joe heard a lady say that Eve was about as close to being a saint as anybody could be on this earth. He thought about it and he believed that was true. He really hurt at the thought of her being sick, and the thought of her dying was almost all he could bear.

One morning at breakfast, Chris Oberlin was worried. "Joe, you and I have got to help Uncle Ed all we can."

Joe felt hurt. "Dad, I'm working as hard as I can, and he says I'm doing a good job."

"Oh, no, I don't mean that, Joe. You're doing fine there. We have to help him because he's hurting." Joe looked at his father inquiringly as he continued. "Eve isn't good. I'm afraid she isn't going to make it. The doctors are doing everything they can for her, but we need to help Uncle Ed. The thought of losing Eve is a lot harder for him to deal with than it would be for him to think about dying himself."

"What can we do, Dad?"

"As gently as possible and in a way he can't notice it, let him know how much we care about him and try to find things to interest him whenever we can. You can do it a lot as his business partner, and I can do it some as we farm together. Yet, I'm wondering if we can't find other things to spark a little bit of interest. Have you talked to him at all about airplanes? It might be that he'd get to talking about airplanes and some of his past, and it would take him off the all-day and all-night thinking about Aunt Eve."

"I'll try, Dad."

The next day, as they were working the abscess on a steer, Joe looked out the barn window at the clear sky and inquired, "What's it like to fly?"

Ed smiled. "It's a whale of a lot of fun, but you have to be on the look-out every second because if you aren't you can easily get killed."

"I wasn't talking about flying in combat where somebody might shoot you; I was talking about just flying. I've never been off the ground. Can you see lots of things from the air that you can't see down here?"

"Lots of things. You can see the rivers, the high ground, the low ground, the sandy ground, the heavy ground, and you can see where people are and where they're going. It looks like Toyland when you look down. When I said you had to be watching out all the time or you might get killed, I wasn't talking about combat. I was talking about if you climb too fast and stall, you can crash into the ground, and if you're not careful of other airplanes around, you can run into each other. Remember, you can't hear anything and you can't see every direction. You can see ahead and above, but you can't see down very well unless you lean clear over, and if your head is above a wing, you can't see straight down. You have to watch your gauges to make sure you have plenty of fuel, and sometimes, you have to watch your instruments because what you feel and what is actually happening may not be the same. It's exciting and it's fun. You have to have a feel for it, but more and more it's getting to be a science as we get bigger planes and new instruments. I haven't been doing much flying, but sometime maybe we could rent a plane and I could take you up. Then we could talk about it a lot better."

Joe's excitement went right through the ceiling. "Could you really? That would be absolutely the most exciting thing I could think about doing!"

Ed stopped his work, looked at Joe, and grinned. "That's a promise."

#

As the weeks went by, Aunt Eve was obviously getting weaker. The whole family tried to be upbeat and happy, particularly around Ed, but Joe felt a lump in his throat a lot of the time. Finally, Aunt Eve went to the hospital. Everybody talked about when she would come back, but in their gizzards, they all knew she wouldn't.

Her funeral was a time of inspiration and mourning. During the calling period, it seemed like the whole town and most of the adjoining towns all came to call. Ed held up bravely but was ready to collapse. The rest of the family felt the agony of losing Eve but awe at the number of people that shared the pain.

As they rode home following the after-burial dinner at the church, Chris said to Ed, "We expect you to have your meals with us. We know you're going to want time to think, but you know that we want you at our house all the time that you can spare for us. Annie thinks that you ought to let her clean house for you and is excited about doing it. Whatever you work out is fine with us."

Ed answered sadly. "Thanks to all of you. I don't want to . . ." for the first time, his chin quivered, "be underfoot, but I need you very much."

No one said anything. Annie, who was sitting on Ed's left, squeezed his hand in hers, and Joe, who was sitting on the other side, put his hand on Ed's shoulder and squeezed it.

In the next weeks, Joe noticed that his dad was having a number of conversations with Uncle Ed and seemed to be pushing him about something while Ed seemed to be quite undecided.

#

It was about a month after this when Joe was taking care of the injured animals that he heard a distant rumble that expanded into a roar. At first, he thought it was a car coming down the road, and then he realized it wasn't on the road. He put down his tools and ran out of the barn to see a yellow airplane coming low over the barn. It circled back and forth, wiggling its wings. Then it went down to the far end of the pasture field, came down, landed, and taxied up toward the barn.

Joe ran toward the airplane in time to see the engine cut, the door drop open, and Uncle Ed climb out of a Taylor Cub.

"Joe, this is my new airplane. I decided instead of renting one, I'd get one. We can cut one side out of the old chicken house and keep it there. We won't have to go away for me to give you that ride I promised you."

Joe was solemn for a minute. "I thought we were all too poor to buy anything big."

Ed grinned. "Joe, we are, but so is everybody else. Your dad heard about this company over by Ft. Wayne that had an airplane with a bad engine, and they were going to have an auction. Your dad figured that nobody would have any money to buy it, particularly with a bad engine, and we might be able to darn near steal it. I went to the auction and bid, bought it for less than a couple cows, and hunted around for engine parts until I got one put together that's as good as new and now we have an airplane. If we watch our pennies to buy gas and I remember what I learned during the war and read up on all the new things, we can fly and do it safe and cheap."

"How about a hop right now?"

Ed grinned. "Got a half a tank, let's get in. First, I'll have to show you how to pull the prop to get it started. You be careful. Stand back so it doesn't hit you."

A few minutes later, they were taking off. Joe felt a lurch in his stomach as they took off and a lot more as the light Taylor Cub bounced in the updrafts and currents. However, Joe was too excited to let his stomach bother him. He watched their house diminish to dollhouse size as they climbed. He was excited to see the roads and even the cow paths in the pastures. Everything looked like a toy land. He could see so many useful things like the parts of fields that were heavy ground and the parts that were sandy, or spots in the cornfields where it needed a tile ditch. In a few minutes, he could see how much field work the neighbors had completed and which farms were neat next to the road and messy farther back. As they descended to land, Joe felt like he was coming home to a whole new world.

#

A few weeks later, as the senior Oberlins were having lunch together, Chris was thoughtful. "I think the airplane is helping. Have you noticed how those two have made that old chicken house into a decent hanger? And they find a lot of excuses to take to the air?"

Mary smiled. "Yes, and have you noticed that Joe's bedroom has Ed's flying books in it? He seems to have memorized all the airplane parts. If you watch him sometimes when nobody is looking, you see him pushing his feet back and forth as if they're on rudders and leaning from one side to the other as if they're in a bank to turn?"

Chris wiped his mouth with a napkin. "I sure have."

"I suspect that while we all think we're doing this for Ed it may be Joe who's getting the biggest thrill."

"Might be. They're still putting their work first. It's interesting how things work out. It seems that whenever anything that is just unbearably bad happens, some good things come along to follow it up. We're lucky. Ed follows all the rules. He records every hour in the air, including every hour of instruction for Joe. He reads all the regulations and the rules. He told me that, very shortly, he thinks Joe is going to be ready to solo. Won't that be great?"

Mary beamed. "That is wonderful."

It was a week after that when Joe soloed. A month later, Chris sat down with his stern-father expression to talk with Joe.

"Joe, I think it's great that you're flying, but some things have to change. The cow quit giving as much milk as she did. I noticed that on the days you fly she always gives less milk. I think you're flying too low over the pasture field. I also noticed that the goats knocked down their fence one day when you were flying. I suspect that you frightened those goats. Furthermore, I've not had any reports, but if you do that kind of thing around the town, I think it's probably illegal, but more particularly, you're going to make a lot of friends mad at us. Has Uncle Ed seen you doing any of this low flying?"

"I don't know."

"You better talk to him about it because he has a good sense of safety. I think he'll agree with me, but safety or not, we can't afford to have the animals frightened. Those we're trying to fatten up won't gain weight and the cow won't give milk. We just can't have it."

"Yes, sir."

Later that day, Chris expressed his concerns to Ed. Ed was philosophical. "Hadn't noticed. Not surprised. Any kid worth his salt feels his oats and has to try the limits. He's a good kid. He wouldn't do it to hurt anybody. He won't do it anymore. You know, I think that's a sign that he's going to be a crackin' good pilot. Good pilots can't resist seeing what that airplane will do."

#

Joe began to feel a new sense of pride about being in a partnership. It first showed up at the sale barn when he noticed a pen bearing their partnership initials, R & O. They now had a special pen at the sale barn for their animals. They also picked up another fringe benefit. One day someone drove in six nice-looking, young steers. Since they would fit with some injured steers that they had cured and they had a little extra pasture, Joe put a low bid on them figuring that the competition would run up the price to full market value, but he bought them because nobody else bid.

He asked a friend to look at them and the friend smiled wryly. "There is nothing wrong with them. You just shot them sitting." Then it dawned on him, everybody in that sale barn figured that, if Joe or Ed bid on anything, something was wrong with it. This actually happened four or five times when they bought quite good animals at very low prices just because they bid on them. They didn't quite know whether to be proud of it or ashamed of it, but it sure did help their business.

#

As Amy Gibbons and Sarah Hughes walked out of science class, Amy looked at Joe walking alone lost in thought and said to Sarah, "I thought you were going with Charlie Fishbauch."

"I am."

"I hear you let Joe Oberlin walk you home after school last night."

"I did. I figure Charlie wouldn't care. He was at basketball practice, and no one would think of Joe as competition."

Amy looked again at Joe. "I can see your point. Charlie is the best-looking and most-popular boy in school. I don't see how the star of the basketball team could look at anybody like Joe as competition, but I hear Charlie is mad as hops about it."

"He couldn't possibly be. Joe is shy. We didn't even walk close to each other."

"I heard Charlie say he's going to beat Joe up."

"He wouldn't. He's so much bigger and stronger than Joe. He'd be looked at as a bully."

"I think he will. He always gets his way. He almost always wins, but he's not a good loser. Have you noticed when we're losing a ballgame he gets mad and fouls out?"

"Yes."

"Well, he's really mad."

"He'll get over it. When he cools down, he'll realize Joe is no competition. Joe's not in his league."

"Sarah, if you think so little of Joe, why did you let him walk you home."

"He's harmless, and I might get a ride in that airplane."

#

That evening, Joe had barely left the school grounds when Charlie Fishbauch walked up to him, grabbed the front of his shirt, and lifted him off the ground.

"You're yellow," Charlie growled, as he slapped Joe's face.

Joe said nothing.

"You're yellow," Charlie said again, as he slapped Joe.

Then Charlie bellowed, "You're yellow!" as he slapped Joe as hard as he could.

Joe couldn't get much leverage with his feet barely touching the ground, but he hit Charlie in the jaw as hard as he could.

Charlie was startled. You just don't hit Charlie Fishbauch; he was the school hero.

With rage, Charlie dropped Joe and cut loose with a barrage of rights and lefts. Joe tried to fight back, but his lips were bleeding and eyes were blurring when Charlie tackled him.

They went down in a heap and Charlie locked his powerful legs around Joe in a scissor hold and squeezed until Joe was in agony.

"Give up?" snarled Charlie.

Joe, barely able to speak, gasped, "Nice day, isn't it?"

A crowd had gathered and hearing Joe's response, they moved in and stopped the fight.

Charlie appeared untouched, but Joe was a bloody mess. The Osgood boys helped Joe mop up most of the blood and walked with him to the telephone office where he called his dad to pick him up.

Joe's head throbbed. He had been humiliated. The whole school would know. It was painful being overlooked, but now he was the disastrous loser in a real fight. The humiliation was so intense Joe wanted to die.

Chris Oberlin's blood pressure surged when he saw Joe.

"Our family doesn't get into fights. What happened?"

"I lost."

"I can see that. How did it start?"

"Charlie picked me up by the shirt and started slapping me."

"Why?"

"I suppose it was because I walked Sarah Hughes home after school."

"What happened after he slapped you?"

"After he called me yellow three times and slapped me three times, I hit him."

Chris paused, reflected, and looked straight into his son's eyes. "I don't blame you."

"Thanks, Dad."

#

At home, his parents gave him first aid and put him to bed with a beefsteak on his eye. Annie ran down to get Uncle Ed and was sent to bed before the adults began to converse.

Chris Oberlin was furious. "I'm going to school in the morning and raise Cain."

Ed was calm. "It won't do any good. It didn't happen on school property."

"Then I'll go to the sheriff."

"They're kids. You'll look like a poor loser. If they did do something and Charlie didn't get to play in the tournament, the whole town would be down on you and Joe."

"A bully beats my son bloody and you want me to do nothing?"

"Yes."

"Why? How can you be so calm?"

"Because Joe won."

"What are you saying? Didn't you see him? He's a bloody mess. He was beaten up."

"Yes, he was, but he won."

Mary spoke up. "What are you saying, Ed?"

"Just add it up. Everyone knows that Charlie is bigger, stronger, and quicker than Joe is. A bunch of kids saw Charlie start the fight, so Charlie goes from school hero to bully.

"Joe proved he wasn't yellow and didn't give up, so he proved he has guts and sheds his identity as a nice little nobody. That bunch of schoolmates who came out here this evening didn't just want to see what he looked like; they wanted to support Joe. I'll bet Charlie had a lonely evening."

Chris was thoughtful. "Joe won't take it that way. He'll see it as more proof that he's a loser."

"At first, maybe, but all of us have told him he handled it well. In the long run, he'll see it like we do.

Mary was weeping. "But in the short run, how much does one kid have to take?"

Chris put his arm around Mary. They both looked at Ed.

Ed smiled. "That kid's a winner. He has what it takes. All this bad stuff will make him strong. He is lucky to learn so much about the downside of life early. It will make his life richer."

Mary wiped her eyes. "Ed, you are wise."

"No, Mary, I'm not. It's the way life is. Look over at the woods. Which is the best tree? It's that tall oak. It's so straight and strong.

"I've been watching it for years. It's that way because it grew up through the brambles and it had to stretch and struggle through those thorny bushes for its place in the sun. Joe is a sapling in the brambles."

Chapter III
1 9 3 6
G r o w t h

As the months went by, they continued to get more animals. Ed's farm was crowded. They rented all the pasture that Chris Oberlin could spare. Too many animals for their land could end their progress.

It was at the end of dinner, Joe and Annie were clearing the table, when Ed Riley put down his coffee cup and spoke out. "I need to have a conference with the whole family."

When they all sat down together, Ed was enthusiastic. "Eve had an insurance policy, and I have kept that money for the right time. The Harkin farm is badly run-down, but when Mr. Harkin was alive fifteen years ago, it was probably the best farm in the county. The ditch is backed up and most of the fields have a lot of brush and weeds in them. Mrs. Harkin died; her heirs are in the city and they want cash. They're going to auction it.

"It's a big farm — 480 acres. It's laid out in the most unique way with forty-acre fields coming up to the ditch that goes right straight down the middle. Most of the fences are still good, and each one of those fields opens up onto the ditch so that when they are in pasture, the animals can drink out of the ditch.

"The problem is it's too wet. I've checked with the County Drainage Board and they say that the ditch that the water is backing in from is going to be cleaned out next year or the year after. That means that it can be drained again. I'm willing to loan the money from Eve's insurance policy to the partnership to buy that farm. I don't think it will sell for more than twenty-five dollars an acre. That means $12,000 could buy that 480 acres. I don't see how we could lose much money on it, and since we don't have to borrow it, I think it's worth a try. You're doing better, Chris, or I'd offer to loan it to you. I know you don't need it. I think this is an opportunity.

Chris Oberlin was deep in thought, slowly turning his iced tea glass with his thumb and forefinger. Mary was listening with complete attention and a trace of eagerness. Annie was, as usual, bubbling with enthusiasm. Joe could only think of them being poor, and poor people didn't buy big farms.

"I'll charge the partnership interest and put up what money it takes. The barn needs some attention. That old Mr. Harkin was one smart cookie. He made the barn so you can bring the hay in with a buck rake, pull it up, and drop it down in the center. Then the cattle eat in from the sides. It has hanging gates that move in. The sheds around the outside protect the cattle, the hay is in the middle and you don't have to fork it down. When Mrs. Harkin rented it out, her tenants didn't keep it clean and it's a mess, but when Mr. Harkin was alive, he fed more cattle with less work than any man I ever knew.

"We have one other thing going for us. It would cost a fortune to clean up all those overgrown fields, but Joe's goats have shown that they can do the job. We could rotate those pastures; put horses in first to eat things down, then cattle in to eat them down some more, then the sheep in to eat them down even more. When it gets down to brush, we'll put the goats in. The goats ought to eat all the little brush and everything but the saplings; those saplings ought to come out pretty easy. I can see Joe down there with Bingo pulling them out. I think we can take that farm back to being one of the best in the county."

Joe said nothing. Everybody thought a little while, and then Chris spoke. "Ed, you're taking all the risk. You think that's fair to you?"

"Yes, it's fair. The only thing you said wrong was when you said 'you' 'cause I think 'us'."

Chris smiled, Mary got a tear in her eye, and Annie kissed Ed on the cheek. Joe swallowed and said nothing.

When the auction came, somebody else bid $12,000, but Ed got it for $12,500.

The horse, cattle, sheep, and goat rotation worked. Joe spent the next summer with Bingo in his heavy harness and a log chain on the single tree. Joe and the big Shire soon knew what to do without much talking. Bingo would walk right up to a sapling and stop. Joe would flip the chain around the sapling and then flip the end of the chain back over itself, hold on to it, and say, "Pull,

Bingo." Bingo would pull and the sapling would come out. Joe would then flip the chain off the uprooted sapling and say, "Okay, Bingo." The big horse would move without guidance to the next sapling. Sometimes, when the saplings were tall, they would swish his rear, but Bingo would never bolt. He was always patient. When they tired, Joe would go to the ditch so Bingo could drink and rest. Sometimes, when Bingo finished his drink, he would rub his head affectionately against Joe.

Fortunately, the saplings had only grown up over the last few years and none of them were too big for Bingo. Some of them made him pull hard, but he did the job. After grubbing the saplings out of a field, Joe, sometimes with the help of one of the Osgood kids, would gather them up and pile them up for burning. After a few weeks of drying, they burned well and field after field returned to productivity. Their rotation grazing actually increased the quality of the grass.

#

Annie worked hard to get her jobs done early. "Mom, may I take a drink and snack out to Joe?"

"Sure."

"I'll help awhile and come home with him."

"Be careful of that big horse."

"I will."

Her mother smiled. She had noticed dried horse sweat on Annie's hand-me-down slacks following earlier trips to see Joe.

"Hi, Joe."

"Hi, Annie."

"Brought you iced tea and two pieces of cake."

"Thanks."

"I'll help you till you are ready to go."

"I thought you would."

"You always see through me. It's worth two pieces of cake just to ride Bingo to the barn.

"Joe, do you think *Lil Abner* is like real life?"

"Sort of. It's real funny. I think it's the best comic strip."

"Some kids call you Carcass-cooker, the Skunk Works, and some call you Lonesome Polecat."

"I know."

"Do you care?"

"Not much. People laughed at the Wright brothers."

"I like comic strips because of what they do for us."

"Like what?"

"Like how when we put our fingers on each other's noses when we say something serious — like they do in the funny papers."

"All kids play games like that."

"But not all families do. Mom and Dad and Uncle Ed all do it to us sometimes and that's special family."

"It is fun when they do that."

"I even saw Mom do it to Dad."

"It's fun, but please don't do it when anyone can see it or I'll be Lonesome Polecat forever."

Joe unhitched Bingo and hoisted Annie to where she could pull herself up on the giant horse's back.

Annie tilted her nose up. "I'm rich. I feel like the Queen of England."

"Anyone who can plop her bottom down into horse sweat and feel like a queen will always be rich."

"Joe, we really are rich. The only thing we don't have is money."

#

The next spring when the giant dredge came up the county ditch dropping the water four feet, Joe and Ed were present. When it came by the end of their private ditch, they were able to get the operator to open the slug that had accumulated where their ditch went into the county ditch. Joe, with his gumboots and shovel, dug a channel on into their own ditch. The water pressure was such that with the sharp drop it began to clean itself. Within a couple of days, the old tile drains that went into the fields were above water.

That night at dinner there was good feeling. Ed summed it up. "By George, we won."

After dinner, Annie and Joe walked Uncle Ed home. On the way back, Annie was wistful. "Joe, if you keep going, you're going to be rich. You own half of lots of animals and half a farm and you're only seventeen years old."

"The war scare in Europe has made prices go up, but really, I'm a failure."

"Why do you think that? I don't think so at all."

"Look at it this way, Annie. I'm getting better, but I'm a lousy athlete. The kids don't like me much. I never get elected to anything. The only things I succeed at are when my family helps me."

"You can fly; none of the other kids can."

Joe kicked a rock in the road. "Uncle Ed did that."

Annie danced in front of him. "The kids in my grade think you're great."

"You did that. Everybody likes you."

Annie shook her head. "Joe, do you enjoy looking at yourself as a flop?"

"No, but you have to see it like it really is." Joe swatted a mosquito on his cheek. "I'd trade my animals and land in a minute if I could be on a team or be popular like you."

"Don't be discouraged, Joe," Annie said in a compassionate voice. She took his hand. "You're growing tall. I heard one of the teachers call you a late bloomer. Anyway, your little sister thinks you're wonderful. Uncle Ed, Mom, and Dad think so, too. We know you best. Give the others time, and they'll catch on."

"You know, Annie, some things are changing. It's taking me a little time to get used to being tall. I still bump my head a lot, but when I run with the guys, I'm not the slowest any more and nobody pushes me around much. There's something else. I don't know how long I'll be around. I keep having this dream about a plane; everything is going well, and then there is a huge yellow light, it spirals down, and everything stops. Mom, Dad, and Uncle Ed say don't worry about it. They say everybody has silly dreams sometimes. Other than that, life couldn't be much better."

"Every dog has his day, but I don't want you to be like the others. I like it when you worry about things because I know you'll figure out what's best and I don't have to bother."

"You little parasite."

"What's a parasite?"

"That's a critter that lives off another critter's blood."

"I live well, but I'll take my turn."

"You already do. An engine is no good without a spark plug."

"Thank you, Joe. I'll really miss you when you go to Purdue."

BOOK II

Chapter IV
December 1941
War

The flag hung limp against its pole at the headquarters of Kelly Field. It was hot, sticky hot. First Lieutenant Joe Oberlin could feel the sweat trickle between his shoulder blades and down his spine. He stood at parade rest with nineteen other officers and forty aviation cadets soon to be second lieutenants all waiting to receive their wings. There was starting to be some action on the speaker's platform; the ceremonies would soon begin.

Joe felt good. The best he had ever felt in his life. He had steadily become more athletic at Purdue where he studied agriculture and had taken R.O.T.C. with all the elective time put into aviation classes.

Since getting his commission the previous June, a horse cavalry unit made up of black soldiers had been his first duty. He worked with them, developed a great rapport, and toughened up. He really liked those black cavalrymen and suspected they liked him, too. Maybe it was because he expected to do things with them and didn't expect them to do things for him. It had come as a real shock out of the blue when his earlier request for the Army Air Corps materialized. Just after receiving his early promotion to first lieutenant, they pulled him out to the Air Corps. His flying hours racked up through high school and the university let him by-pass primary and go straight to basic along with a handful of other officers with similar flying experience.

For the most part, adjustment to the army had been easy. At first, the swearing had bothered him, but after he recovered from the initial shock, he came to look at it as soldier communication and not true profanity.

It was at basic where he met Crole. Because they were the same height, regulations required them to march together whenever they marched. Crole had nothing but contempt for Joe. He considered Joe to be the classic country bumpkin, stumble bump, who was too square to live life and too much of a bore to be caught with. Joe was not fond of Crole, who was what some of his cronies described as a woman-chasing, booze-guzzling hotshot. Much to their regret, the army constantly threw them together.

It had been unclear whether the friendship started because Joe, out of compassion, had so many times put the drunken Crole to bed and thus averted his being washed out of flight training or because of Crole's decision to try to make a human being out of Joe. Their relationship had evolved from contempt, to tolerance, to acceptance, to genuine friendship.

Crole, a good athlete, had watched Joe's movements — particularly his marching. During one workout, he put chalk on the heels of Joe's shoes and told him he didn't want to see any marks on the chalk. Joe, who had been one of the slower men in the outfit, was now the fastest in the 440 and could hold his own at any distance. The day he beat Crole in a 440 run was a day of sheer joy for Joe and a mixture of pride and fierce annoyance on the part of Crole.

As they continued to wait, Joe felt gratitude for Crole, for Uncle Ed's training, kindness, and belief in him when he showed so little promise. He thought of Aunt Eve always finding the good in everybody, which probably had been instrumental in his finding good things in Crole that led to this friendship. This led to cheering thoughts about Annie and his parents.

"Attention!"

They all jerked from parade rest to attention at the command of Col. Parks, the base commander. "We will now have the national anthem."

The base band pounded out the "Star-Spangled Banner" with an enthusiasm that covered a minimum of talent, and Joe felt his usual goose bumps as he recounted so many things that the music represented.

As the program droned along, Joe wondered how long the dull speech would be. He felt alone. There were so many beautiful wives and sweethearts there to pin on wings. Joe had never really had any ongoing interest in a girl. He had had lots of dates, but none of them seemed to have the right chemistry. He had really hoped that his parents could come and his mother would pin his wings on, but his dad had broken his leg the week before and Mother and Uncle Ed would have to stay home to keep things going. He would be one of the few that the Commanding Officer would pin the wings on. From where he was standing, he couldn't see who the speaker was. He hoped they would be mercifully brief.

His attention came sharply back as the colonel announced, "It's my pleasure to introduce our speaker of the day. I had the pleasure of serving with him in the Allied Expeditionary Force of World War I where we were fellow pilots, and he was one of the best who flew. This Double Ace chose to leave the service after the war, and we didn't get reacquainted until a few weeks ago when I immediately asked him to speak to this group. I can assure you the speech will be brief, but let me tell you, listen to every word. There's no man in this world more qualified to tell you graduating pilots what you need to know. It is my pleasure to introduce to you one of the great surviving combat pilots of this world, Captain Ed Riley of the Allied Expeditionary Force of World War I."

Joe sucked in his breath, as he saw the form of Uncle Ed rise to the podium.

Ed Riley deadpanned. "Thank you, Colonel, you overrate me. It was a pleasure to serve with that great group of men, one of the best of whom was you. Now, to you men who are about to fly in combat for your country, I have a few things to say, and I hope you'll listen.

"Number One: Take care of your ground crew; your life depends on them. They don't get enough credit. Let them know you appreciate what they do. Let them know you know your life depends upon them. Do everything you can to look after them.

"Number two: Tend to business. Fighting the enemy is your business. Hot-piloting, show-off flying, trying to impress the other troops, the other pilots, or the civilians kills people — doesn't make you any better and shows you don't have your priorities where they ought to be.

"Number three: Get along with the other pilots. Their life depends upon you; your life depends upon them. It doesn't matter who gets the rank, it matters who wins the war.

"Number four: Don't dogfight. Try to get higher and come in on them out of the sun. General Chenault's right, our P-40s can't tangle with the Zeros, but the Zeros go down easy when you hit them, so shoot them and keep right on going — don't dogfight. When it comes to the Germans, remember, they've been fighting for years. Those Kraut ME-109s and Faulkwolfs are good airplanes, and they've been flying them in combat for a long time.

Until you get more experience and until we get better planes, shoot and keep right on going.

"Number five: Look around all the time. Remember, the enemy will always try to hit you when you least expect it. A good pilot has his head on a swivel; he never quits looking.

"Number six: Watch how you handle your booze or don't handle it at all. I know lots of good pilots think they need to hang one on every so often and I can understand it. If you have to, wait till the weather is going to be socked in for a couple days and you have plenty of time to sober up. You take it from me, it takes every bit of quickness you have. If you're either carrying alcohol or fighting a hangover, it slows you up. It may cost you your life, but worse than that, it may cost the life of a buddy whom you should have been taking care of. If it does, it will haunt you till you die."

Joe felt tremendous pride in Uncle Ed — so brief, so right, so kind. He watched the other officers and cadets who were giving their rapt attention to excellent advice and realized that he had had it all his life.

"Number seven: Be careful. Think ahead so you can react the right way when you don't have time to think. Dead pilots and crashed airplanes don't win wars.

"Number eight: We're fighting for the greatest country on earth. We're fighting sick minds leading people who are brainwashed. To do that it takes all you have and a lot you don't have. When it gets to what you don't have, you need to have a faith. Work at it now, so it will carry you when it has to. Work at it now and keep working at it. Thank you." He sat down.

Joe was in shock. So that was it. He'd always wondered, but that was it. Uncle Ed had quit the service and become an alcoholic because something was eating him. Now he knew. He'd either been hung over or drunk when a good friend cashed in, and he felt responsible. Now he knew why Sunday school had included so much talk about drinking and about the forgiveness of a loving God. Somehow, Uncle Ed was now complete in his eyes.

A few minutes later when Joe got his wings, Uncle Ed stepped forward beaming and pinned Joe's wings on. Joe muttered very softly, "You never told me you were an Ace."

"You never asked me, Joe." Then he corked Joe's shoulder with a hard fist, so hard that Joe could barely give him a salute.

C h a p t e r   V
1 9 4 2
C o m b a t

Mud squished up on to Joe's shoes, as he walked toward the CO's tent next to the airstrip. The reluctant jungle gave up part of itself for this base, and when it rained it wanted to take it back. As he entered, the Colonel, who was sitting at his desk, looked up with a friendly face as Joe saluted. The Colonel returned the salute. "You wanted to see me, Joe? What's up?"

Joe was hesitant. "Sir, you've told us several times if any of us had a suggestion you wanted it. I think you said it's going to take the best thoughts of all of us to win this war. I respectfully would like to suggest something that maybe is already being planned, but if it isn't, I would like to suggest it. It may be very high risk, but I would be happy to participate in it."

The Colonel sat rigid in his chair. He looked at Joe with somber eyes. "What is it, Captain?"

"Sir, we've been escorting those medium bombers over the Japanese bases on the north side of New Guinea and taking heavy losses. The Japs are always ready for us and the Zeros are up there at our level, so we can't dive on them and run. We've lost too many bombers and lost too many of our P-40s. We both know that the P-40 is tough, and we know it can dive hard. We also know it can't fight the Zero one on one, and we have to get them where we have the advantage."

The Colonel loosened up slightly. "I know that, Joe. Been thinking hard on it. What is your suggestion?"

"Sir, they seem to always be ready for us, but those Zeros have to take off someplace, some time. My suggestion would be to continue the basic plan of picking up the medium bombers just as they pass over the mountains with the bulk of our fighters. However, if we carefully calculate the times and you let three or four of us take off early, fly at very low altitude, and swing in a circle we could evade any Jap identification. If we hit their airbase just as they are taking off or assembling to take off, we'd either have them on the ground or we could get them when they are climbing when we'd have speed and altitude on them. Now, the problem is after we did that, if they had any planes in the air, it would be a short life expectancy for those of us who went in early. I'm happy to volunteer and I suspect Jenson and Johnson would go with me. I hope I'm not too presumptuous, sir."

The Colonel smiled. "Not at all, Joe. We need this kind of thinking. To tell you the truth, I don't think any of our people thought of that and they should have. Now let's think in terms of time and possibility. I don't know if I could order a man to do it, but you say you'd volunteer and you think a couple of others would. It's worth a shot. I like your thinking and I like your guts. I also like the fact that you shot down a Zero the other day. How did you do it?"

"Well, sir, he was making his turn and I knew he was going to be on my tail, so I did it just like we used to shoot rabbits back in Indiana. I just let fly with a lot of stuff out ahead of him and he flew right into it."

"Good job, Joe. Let's get to a map."

#

Three days later, Joe in his P-40 and two other P-40s piloted by Jenson and Johnson wheeled off the airstrip thirty minutes ahead of anybody else's take-off. It was going to be a near cut thing because they'd have to swing wide and their gasoline would be nip and tuck to get back to the base if they made it. They couldn't have more than one or two swipes over the enemy airfield. If their timing was wrong, they'd have nothing. They flew low to the ground over the land, swung wide out over the water, and came back in at near water level until a few miles from the shore.

When there would be no warning time, they lifted up to get some altitude, dove on the base, and found themselves in luck. The Zeros had apparently just received the warning of incoming aircraft nearing the mountains. They were taxiing and lining up at the other end of the runway. Joe barked on the radio, "Jenson, right behind me; Johnson behind Jenson. Get them on the ground if you can. We'll make one pass at them head-on, turn right around, and try to pick off anything that is taking off."

Joe lowered down and cut loose into the line of Zeros, concentrating quickly on one, another, another, another, another, and pulled up yelling, "You guys pick out the ones I missed. I'm coming in the other way as soon as you pull up. It's for sure there will be two or three trying to take off. We need to get them; we don't want them on our behinds."

As he pulled up and looped around, he could hardly believe his eyes. The Zeros, without self-sealing gas tanks and being full of fuel, had leaked gasoline all over and tracer bullets had ignited it. There were five or six in flames. Two were trying to take-off, as others diverted around trying to avoid the fire of Jenson and Johnson. Joe dove in with a burst at the first one just as its wheels left the ground. It exploded in the air. He pulled up, came sharply down on the tail of the other one who was struggling to climb and it also burst into flame. Joe peeled around, looked back to see Johnson and Jenson strafe the remaining planes and then pull up and each knock-off a climbing Zero.

Joe barked out, "Four out of the air and a mess on the ground. We'll see if we can get home and save our rears."

At full throttle, they climbed toward the mountains, were able to make it over, and landed at the airstrip with barely enough gasoline.

It was 1900 hours that evening when the Colonel's orderly entered Joe's tent. "Captain, the Colonel wants to see you on the double."

Joe hurried over to the Colonel's tent, entered the door, and saluted. The Colonel was smiling. "Look at these recon photos. They confirm four aircraft shot down out of the air as you see the distance of the crash sites from the end of the runway. They also confirm six Zeros destroyed on the ground and six others apparently substantially damaged. When the Japs catch onto this tactic, they'll have constant airborne cover. Do you think there's a chance we could pull it off again tomorrow morning before they wise up? This was your idea and it worked. I hate to ask you to volunteer twice, but it's for sure it won't work more than a day, if it works a day."

"Sir, I would be happy to volunteer. We have seen that other airstrip from the air. I suspect Johnson and Jenson would be willing to try it again, but I don't think there's a prayer of being this lucky again. They surely have some word already."

"I don't doubt that, but the Japs historically are slow to change their plans. It's so obvious what they ought to do that it won't last long, but I think there's a chance. I won't ask you to go. I won't order you to go, but if you think there's a reasonable chance, I'm all for it."

"I'll go, sir. I'll ask Johnson and Jenson."

The next morning as they came in from the sea following the same plan, they rose up near the shoreline and saw the other airbase. Much to their surprise, they saw much the same thing but not as many airplanes.

Joe was excited. "There they are. We'll have to keep a sharp eye; they're not as thick as last time."

Again they dove in and wreaked havoc among the Zeros on the ground. When they turned around, Joe was in the lead and shot down one Zero as it was lifting off the runway. Jenson and Johnson each picked off another, but the ground damage was less than that of yesterday.

Joe spoke on the radio. "Let's keep our eyes peeled. All the birds weren't in the nest; we're in for it."

They headed straight for home. Much to their amazement, they couldn't pick out any Zeros on their tail. As they climbed near the peak of the mountain range, Joe all of a sudden saw a shadow pass over his cockpit as he realized something that none of the three of them had picked up was diving on them out of the sun.

"They're on our tails guys; give it all you have and head for home." A second later, he felt a shudder as something hit his airplane and the Zero went on in front of him. He pulled back, gave it a burst from his remaining ammunition, thought he saw some damage, but felt jolted. He called out, "Johnson, Jenson, you okay?"

"Roger. We're both okay, but you're showing smoke."

"You guys hightail it for home. I'll make it as far as I can. If I have to hit the silk, I'll find my way out of the jungle. I hope I'm not on the Jap's turf."

"We'll stay with you."

"You will not. This is an order. You go home fast. It doesn't do us any good to lose three airplanes if we could settle for one."

"Roger, Wilco, sir."

Joe, still making full airspeed, noted what appeared to be a slight drop in oil pressure and muttered, "Oh-oh." As he passed over the mountains, the oil pressure dropped rapidly and very shortly his engine froze. He decided to glide as far as he could and then bail out. As he was gliding, he recognized not too far ahead some open spaces that showed a native village with what looked like it might be a church.

He threw back his canopy and jumped out. As he guided his chute as much as he could toward the opening, it was clear he wasn't going to make it. He caught in a tree scratching him up some but also breaking the fall, so he felt very little as he touched the ground. He squirmed out of the harness, pulled the chute from the tree, scraped off some dirt, and buried it. Then he started toward the houses and what he could now see was a hut with a cross on top. He had gone a short distance when he saw the curious faces of villagers and what appeared to be a priest in the frock of a monk. The villagers were neither hostile nor friendly, but big eyes watched closely, as they wondered what had fallen from the sky. He walked through the natives to the priest and inquired, "Do you speak English?"

The priest smiled. "I was afraid you were Japanese. I come from Australia and the Japanese fly over a bit. I've been afraid of what would happen if the Japanese take this territory, as I have a small flock of good Catholics."

"Let's hope they don't take this territory. How far away are they?"

"My people report to me that they are about forty miles to the northeast, but they send patrols over very close. None have reached the village, but if they keep coming closer, they will in a few days."

Joe looked at the priest. "Father, I need to get back to my base so that I can fly again, and I need a little medical attention to this shoulder. I think something went through it when that Zero shot me down."

The priest looked at the shoulder. "Yes, you have a neat bullet hole that goes in and out. It looks like it went through the muscle. I will give you first aid. We have a young man here who will make a fine guide. He speaks a little English. I will ask him to guide you toward the coast. It will be a close thing, as the Japanese are putting patrols on our side of the river all the time."

"Thank you, Father."

Chapter VI
A Challenging
Walk Home

As Joe followed Koo down the trail toward the river, he felt optimistic. The priest had bandaged his shoulder, fed him well, given him a container of cooked rice, and a bottle of water. He looked at Koo, a boy probably sixteen with a magnetic smile, abiding Catholic faith, and a large machete. Joe looked at his 45, his two spare clips of ammunition, and his survival knife. He thought, *If we hit a Jap patrol, we're not much of an army.*

Koo's English was limited, but his smile was illuminating and his eyes were keen.

Joe smiled at Koo. "We have to keep a sharp look out so we don't get killed and are able to tell our people what the Japanese are doing."

Koo grinned at him. "Japanese, bad guys. Jesus people good guys."

Joe grinned back. "You got it right, Koo."

Koo moved at a pace one might call a silent trot. It was a little fast for Joe's most rapid walk. Koo had decided that the smart thing to do with his clumsy, heavy-shoed ward was to trot well ahead.

The first day went without event, but mid-morning of the second day, Koo froze, quietly came back to Joe, and pushed him to the side of the trail into the bushes and whispered, "Watch." They stood still for a long time, and then Koo slowly motioned for Joe to come forward. They looked across the river and could see a great deal of activity. The Japanese were there in some force, apparently assembling a number of boats for a river crossing. Joe, having seen the maps before he left, recognized that the principal ground threat to their airbase and to the New Zealand and Australian troops on the ground would be the Japanese crossing upriver and descending from the north. The river's width toward the mouth formed a substantial defensive barrier and gave the Allies some flexibility as to where to meet an attack.

As Koo and Joe moved closer to get a good observation, Joe spoke softly, "Look at the wooden boats pulled up on the shore next to their supplies and ammunition. They are building up for a lot more patrols. The boats have outboard motors. See all those fuel cans?"

They watched the Japanese for an hour noting the heaviness of the marsh grass where they were camped. Joe was surprised. "They have only sentries and no defensive works. They have no fear of attack."

As he watched the dust and the brownness of the grass, he asked Koo, "Isn't it unusually dry here?"

Koo thought a minute and ran the words through his mind a couple of times. "Oh, very dry here. We careful. Fire bad when things so dry."

Joe smiled. "Koo, are you up to a little mischief before we get to the coast?"

Koo looked at him with a blank expression. "What mischief? What is mischief?"

Joe was solemn. "What do you think would happen if the grass caught on fire and went down toward the Japanese with their fuel cans and boats? The wind is out of the north today, and if it holds until we get across the river, we might be able to start a nice fire that would give them a lot of trouble and get back before they found out what happened."

Koo sucked his lower lip under his shiny upper teeth and knit his brow for a little while then grinned broadly. "I can find a small boat. When it's dark we can cross the river."

Joe smiled at Koo. "I have some matches in my survival kit."

Koo didn't understand it but realized this funny man sometimes said things that didn't make much sense.

When they cut back from the river, Joe took a stick and drew Koo a map in the ground. "We will start fires up wind from the boats just far enough away that the Japanese can't see them spread. We will start bundles of grass burning then drag them in a curve farther south so that when the Japanese retreat from the flames they will be caught in a loop of fire and forced on south. When we get back to our little boat, we're going to paddle as fast as we can past their camp and try to start another fire on the other side. We might trap a bunch of those guys if we don't get shot first."

Koo was excited with the plan. "Japanese bad guys."

As they paddled along the west shore of the river under the cover of darkness, they gave it all they had hoping to be unseen and to get well past the Japanese concentration before the light of the fire would reflect on the water and give them away. Koo was a good paddler. Joe did his best. Their narrow canoe moved rapidly. Their burning bunches of dried grass had worked well. They could see in the distance the fire rising more and more in a giant crescent approaching the Japanese camp.

They moved faster than the spread of the fire and were able, after about half a mile, to cut across the river. They concealed their boat and ran as rapidly as they could inland then to the north to set fires where the flames would join. They were able to get back to the river before the fires gave off enough light to attract attention.

They crossed the river, hid their boat, and got a night's sleep concealed far enough from the river to avoid detection. During the night, they heard gasoline cans and ammunition exploding in the fire.

Joe felt pangs of empathy for the Japanese. They could save themselves from the fire by going into the river, but would their fanaticism make them try to save their equipment and die? The army had trained him about the necessity of killing to save yourself and your buddies and the necessity of winning the war. He understood the realities, but somehow, he couldn't shake the pain he had created. He had to conquer it or it would do him in.

The next morning, they took just enough time to see the charred ruins of the Japanese encampment. They were too far away to see beyond the remnants of the sheds and boats, but it was clear that there would be no supplies there for any military operations. After a quick look and a few notes made by Joe, they started south at their fast walk-trot combination hoping to get back to friendly turf in the next couple of days.

A day later, they were still in apparently uninhabited land, but they noticed more and more tracks where patrols had been walking back and forth. They didn't like what they saw because the footmarks were not similar to the boot tracks farm-boy Joe had noticed from the Anzacs or the GI's. They were clearly Japanese footprints.

The terrain now showed patches that had been cultivated but no natives. They had apparently pulled out in fear of the Japanese or the Allies or both.

Koo's instincts and movements reminded Joe of the kind of skills he'd seen in trained bird dogs back in Indiana. His every sense was alert every second, and he insisted on being fifty to a hundred feet ahead of Joe all the time expecting Joe to follow him. When he left the trail, Joe should leave the trail. Joe, remembering the kind priest's comments about the conversion of his people, thought that Koo's basic skills in the art of jungle warfare honed at an early age would be useful. Koo now stayed off the trail. He had an uncanny ability to find openings through the undergrowth and returned to the trail only when the underbrush was too heavy. He urged Joe to walk on his toes lest the heel marks give them away to observant Japanese eyes.

It was late in the afternoon when Koo froze and pointed. Joe quietly slid up behind Koo. As they looked over to the trail, they saw a Japanese patrol moving ahead of them. Koo and Joe stood frozen until the Japanese patrol was safely on ahead, and then they slowly shadowed them.

Joe whispered to Koo, "This is a pretty safe place to be. It is unlikely there will be another patrol close behind."

Two hours later, Koo again froze and pointed at the patrol. It was clear that they had sighted something ahead of them and they were setting up an ambush. Joe and Koo were slightly above the Japanese. They were able to look in the distance and see a string of men marching directly up the trail toward the concealed Japanese.

It was an Allied patrol made up of Anzacs with an American and an Australian officer in the front and a point man well out ahead of them. Joe signaled to Koo that he was going to get up closer, pulled out his 45, examined it, and slipped it back into his holster. He started to move forward. He glanced at Koo and saw him signing that he was going to go, too. Joe knew he couldn't stop him and fell in behind the stealthy, skillful native, as they moved on toward the Japanese staying behind cover and under brush all the way using the remarkable skills of Koo.

About thirty feet behind the Japanese was as far as they could go with concealment. They watched as the Japanese deployed in a crescent with the ends forward to the sides of the trail so that at the proper time they could fire into the patrol from straight ahead and from both sides. The Japanese officer and his non-commissioned officer had stationed themselves in the center with each of their men taking a concealed position with good cover.

It was apparent that the initial firing would be carnage for the oncoming patrol. As Joe watched, the Japanese officer raised his arm and Joe recognized that the point man would pass on by, apparently to be eliminated later. There would be no warning shots. The patrol's slaughter was imminent. He hoped that the point man was alert and would stop and diagnose the situation before they got him. As they watched the Japanese officer's hand in the air, Joe knew that he was going to have to fire accurately and rapidly. He thought it was somewhat similar to the rabbits in the brush pile except there was no time, and he had to do it with a pistol instead of a rifle.

As the Japanese officer's arm rose slightly, Joe opened fire rapidly hitting the officer, the non-commissioned officer, and two of the Japanese soldiers before sliding down and moving off to the right to the position Koo had established for shooting at the other side. As he slid out of his former position, rifle fire from both sides was ripping into it. When he moved off to the right, he was able to get off three more shots and the rifle fire of the Japanese diminished considerably. There was a short silence, and then Koo tapped him on the shoulder and pointed. He could see movement, as the remaining Japanese soldiers were retreating to the north. One broke into the open and Joe downed him.

Joe heard the bang of a large caliber rifle. It was quite distinguishable from the smaller bore Japanese rifles. The point man was trying to pick off the Japanese stragglers.

When the firing started, the Allied patrol dove for cover. The American officer yelled, "That's a fire fight ahead. I would know the bang of an American 45 anywhere. We better split and move up on each side as quickly as we can." They divided the command, half under the Australian officer, and half under the American, and moved forward rapidly.

Before they arrived at the Japanese position, they heard an American voice boom out. "Take it easy guys, there's nobody up here but a couple of friends. The point man is on ahead, but he seems to be taking good care of himself."

When the patrol arrived, Joe looked at the American officer. "You got any 45 ammo? I just used up my last round."

As they looked around, they found four dead Japanese and several blood trails leading away.

Joe reflected on what he had done. The Japanese had done their duty and he had done his, but he still felt pain. Their families cared about them. He wondered if their pride in having made that sacrifice for the emperor would blot out their pain.

He felt sick when he thought about these things. There was a war on and he had to suck it up and get on with it; if he didn't, he couldn't endure.

Joe walked over to the dead Japanese officer and removed his samurai sword. He then called Koo over, saluted him, and strapped the sword around Koo's waist. Koo showed his magnificent teeth with his enchanting grin. He pulled the sword out and made large sweeping gestures. Not the kind of gestures that you would make in combat, but clearly excited about the weapon as an oversized machete to cut his way through the jungle.

The Australian lieutenant walked up to Joe and saluted him smartly. "Very good of you, sir. Those bloody blokes would have had us for sure without you moving in on them."

Joe responded, "It wasn't as hard as you might think when you have a guide like him," and pointed to Koo. The officer then turned to Koo and saluted. The young native again grinned broadly.

As Joe turned to talk to the American officer, he noticed the Aussie point man returning to the group. He walked up to the Aussie lieutenant. "That was a near thing, sir. I got one and I winged one, but without that Yank officer and his bloody savage we would have all been goners for sure."

The American officer looked hard at Joe. "Aren't you Captain Oberlin?"

"Yeah. And you look familiar."

"I'm Lt. Small. I'm from the MPs on the base. We've had some reinforcements, and the Colonel decided that since the base was fundamentally secure we should rotate officers out with the Aussie patrols to get a better feel of what the Japs were doing."

The Lieutenant looked at Joe. "You're wounded, sir."

Joe looked at his side. "I felt something hit there; I thought it was just a limb. I was in a hurry to get from one position to another."

"You better let me have a look at it." He found a small bore rifle wound on Joe's left side. He put sulfa on it, bandaged it, and then said, "We're about a day's walk from the base. Do you think you can make it?"

"I think I can, but if I can't, that man Koo could probably carry me."

Chapter VII
Transfer

The Colonel was mad, deep-down bitter angry. He looked at his staff and growled, "Can you believe this order from Washington? Here we are struggling in the mud and starved for pilots. We got a good break when Joe made it back, but the doctors say they won't let him fly for six to eight weeks. He has an infection in his second wound. He's doing okay, but that doesn't help our problem now, and look at this order. They are ordering us to send one of our experienced pilots back to consult with them on how to train pilots to deal with the Japanese, and the Zero in particular. We're hurting enough for pilots as it is. We could teach them quick enough when they send them out here. We could spread out our experienced pilots to fly with the greenhorns, but to send one of our best men back now is just plain crap. Nevertheless, it's orders, and in this man's army, orders are orders. Who can we send? Both Johnson and Jenson are good men.

The second in command spoke up. He was an affable guy who'd been a public relations man in New York before entering the army and had a knack for working in people situations. "Maybe this isn't as bad as it might be. Oberlin is out for six to eight weeks anyhow. He's probably well enough to travel, and he is as experienced as any pilot we have. We could ship him off now and for the next six to eight weeks, we wouldn't be any worse off. He has two Purple Hearts and the Air Medal. You've already put him in for the Distinguished Flying Cross for his raids on the Japanese airbases. I'm told that the ground forces have put him in for a Bronze Star for his burning up of the Japanese camp and they're in the process of writing him up for the Silver Star for saving that Aussie patrol. If we get that paperwork together, they'll have to listen to him."

The Colonel was abrupt. "You're right. Furthermore, if we're going to send somebody back there, we had better stack enough medals on him that people will listen to him. Anyway, he's earned it. Anybody with nothing but a pistol who can knock off four Japs, wound a bunch of others, and save a patrol deserves the Silver Star. Let's do it."

Smith, the supply officer and the most thoughtful member of the staff spoke up. "To do that to Joe, who's a good and dog-loyal officer, is a dirty trick. He won't want to cop out over here."

The Colonel smiled then smirked. "That poor officer will just have to suffer; but you're right, it will bother him."

Smith replied, "He's not as shy as you might think."

"Why?"

"Remember Phelps, that over-eager captain from the inspector general's office?"

"Yeah."

"He honked off just about everybody and messed up a lot of common sense operations."

"What about him?"

"Joe never crossed him when he was here, but his next stop was Australia. When he left, Joe told him that in Australia when you finished your drink it was proper to turn the mug upside down."

"So what?"

"In Australia, when you turn your mug upside down you're saying you can whip anybody in the joint!"

Chapter VIII
Rejection in
England

Captain Joe Oberlin entered the office of Tactical Air Evaluation, Southwest Pacific. The place reeked of military bureaucracy, but he saluted the Colonel and reported. Joe had arrived, but the paperwork and his personal records had been lost somewhere.

The Colonel looked at his ribbonless chest. "I asked for a more experienced officer, and they sent me you."

"Sir, my colonel said he was sending the paperwork ahead of me. I was delayed a few days because the flight surgeons wouldn't let me fly."

The Colonel stared at him. "Have you fought Zeros?"

"Yes, sir."

"How do they compare to our P-40s in combat?"

"Sir, we can't dogfight with them. Everything considered, the Zero is a better airplane than ours is. We can out dive the Zero and the P-40 is tough, but the Zero can out climb us, can turn inside of us, and it's faster than we are. I think the P-40 would take a lot more incoming fire than the Zero, but it is so darn hard to get a shot at those Zeros."

The Colonel was still unconvinced. He spoke in a monotone. "I thought they'd send me an officer who had done something. Have you shot any Zeros down?"

"Yes, sir."

"How many?"

"Four."

"Well, that's a little better. What do you think we ought to do?"

"Sir, I think General Chenault is right. Get as high as you can, come in out of the sun, dive down, shoot, and keep right on going. We don't have a prayer if we try to dogfight with them in P-40s."

"What about P-38s? We sent some out there."

"I never flew one, sir. I doubt if we could dogfight with them. They are faster than the P-40 with their twin engines and counter-rotating props. They shouldn't have any torque pulling on them. I think they could hold their own, but I don't know."

The Colonel seemed to Joe to be a little bit bored, a little bit frustrated, and of the desk-bound mentality as he spoke. "Write out your report, and then we'll figure out where to send you for your next assignment."

#

Three weeks later, Joe walked into the Quonset hut that served as the Officer's Club on the fighter base at North Chevington, England. He had arrived the night before and then taken part in gunnery practice the next morning before the rain weathered them out. He'd not had a chance to meet any of the fellow officers and he looked forward to the chance that he might know someone. When the door banged behind him, he shook the rain off his hat and coat and hung them up. He looked around. There were many pilots enjoying singing and drinking and having a general good time. Most were pretty well into their cups, but Joe was relieved because he had just seen the report from the meteorologist. There would be no flying for the next three or four days. Hopefully, they would be over their hangovers before they got back into the cockpits of their P-47s. As he looked around to see if he knew anyone, he heard a shout from the back of the room.

"Holy Moses, there's a sad sack if I ever saw one."

He hadn't heard that voice since they split up the day after they got their wings, and he felt the thrill of Crole's complimentary insult. The voice got even louder. "It's the cube. He's square anyway you look at him. He is the dullest, dumbest farmer you ever saw, and if anybody else says that, they have me to fight." Crole almost jumped over the tables, pushed people out of the way, wrestled his way up to Joe, hit him hard on both shoulders, and gave him a quick jab to the solar plexus.

Crole looked at him. "You look like a shop-worn, flea-bitten, worn-out son of a bitch. Come on over and meet my guys."

Joe looked at the captain's bars on Crole's shoulders. "Congratulations, Crole. They must have been scraping the bottom of the barrel."

Crole grinned. "They had to be or they wouldn't have promoted scum like me. The Air Corps is expanding like mad and they're hard up for pilots over here."

Shortly after enthusiastic introductions, Joe heard the voice of a Colonel Armentrout. Armentrout was the most respected officer on the base. He was Deputy Commander and a West Pointer. He was well known to be both tough and fair.

Armentrout jerked his thumb. "Come join me for a drink, Oberlin. I want to show my respect to the pilot who won the gunnery competition this morning."

"Sir, I didn't know I'd won. Thank you very much."

"Oh shut-up, sit down, and have a drink with me. What do you have?"

"I'd like an orange squash, sir."

"Orange squash? Hell, get something that will put some hair on your chest."

"Sir, I don't drink alcohol."

"How in the hell can you be a soldier if you don't drink alcohol?"

"Sir, it's a religious commitment I made earlier in my life."

"When somebody said square, they must have been talking about you. Have a cigarette."

"No, thank you, sir."

Armentrout, who was well into his cups, curled his lip with disgust. "I suppose you don't screw women either."

"Sir, I follow a system that I worked out. There are some things I plan on saving for marriage."

"Oh shit!" barked Armentrout. "I got to West Point because my pappy won the Congressional Medal of Honor in the Marine Corps, and he told me that anybody who didn't smoke, drink, or screw women was yellow and you could never count on them in combat. I'll not have any of my people put at risk by somebody who doesn't have the guts to fight. Forget about that offer of the drink and get out of my sight."

"Yes, sir."

Joe got up and walked away.

Crole was dumbfounded as he looked at Joe. "He's a good officer. I never saw him like that. They sent you up here to command B Flight. If you get it, you're going to have one tough time because you would be under his wing."

"From what I just heard, looks to me like a sure thing I won't be commanding B Flight.

Joe stayed with Crole. They chatted for another hour or so until Crole was too far in his cups to function. Joe took him to his billet, got him to bed, and stayed with him until he was snoring soundly. Then he went back to his own billet, went to bed, and thought things over. This was not a good situation.

Armentrout was a good officer, a really good officer. None of the pilots Joe had talked with could understand what happened. They'd never seen this before in Armentrout. Joe appeared to be the victim of a real old-fashioned grudge.

Joe didn't get command of B Flight. He was pushed to one side and command of B Flight went to Crole. Joe was grateful that Crole got the command. He had heard that another squadron was coming to share the base and assumed a transfer would be coming.

In the meantime, he was just on the perimeter. He did some training flights, worked out more than usual, and started distance running to stay in shape. It was of some solace to him that some of the other pilots went out of their way to be friendly. Apparently, these were people who listened to Crole who had made a major effort to put in good words about Joe wherever he could.

Joe often ran down the British back roads or through the village running three and four miles at a time. A few pilots joined him, and it gave him great satisfaction to feel his body recovering fully from his wounds.

More than that, it lifted his spirits. Rural England was like a giant garden — rolling hills with lush grass and trees, stone fences, beautiful sheep, cattle, and horses, old stone houses with thatched roofs, an occasional mansion, and the ruins of keeps and castles all came together to remind him of his heritage. Americans raised on Kipling, Dickens, and a host of other English authors couldn't escape a little feeling of coming home as they trotted over the rolling countryside.

He sometimes ran down the main street of the village where he noticed a sign in front of the Methodist Church: *Young Adult Discussions, Sunday Evening at 6:30.* He thought the English were all Church of England; this prickled his curiosity.

The first Sunday after reading the sign, Joe entered the church and saw a circle of young adults sitting with the minister.

The minister rose smiling warmly. "Please join us." He pointed to an empty chair. "We're discussing the letters of Paul. Are you familiar with them?"

"I grew up going to Sunday school. I have read Paul's letters several times, but no one ever adequately understands them, and I'm sure that I understand them less than others do."

"Jolly good. You'll do. Welcome to our group."

As Joe listened to the discussion, he looked around the room. The group comprised of about half males and half females apparently all British except Joe. Some of the males were in uniform, some were in civilian clothing, one civilian had an empty sleeve, another one had what appeared to be an artificial limb coming from his pant leg, while another showed physical frailty that indicated he could not have qualified for the military. Some of the girls were in the uniform of ambulance drivers or other governmental support groups.

Directly across from him sat a tall girl with straight black hair and brown eyes. She sat up very straight, had a beautiful set of white teeth, and when she smiled, the center two upper teeth looked slightly longer than the rest. Joe mused that they were very attractive, but if she were his sister, he would call her Bugs for Bugs Bunny. Because of the way she spoke and sat, he thought any slight variation from perfection would probably bother her.

As the discussion went on, they moved into the business of Paul's attitude toward women. The young lady, who was Bugs in his mind, spoke out with a clarity and analytical chain of thought that he had not heard before.

"His letter saying women should not speak in the Church was directed to only one church where there was a group of very difficult women. At other times, Paul called on women to take leadership roles within the Church. Paul was not anti-women; he was just strongly in favor of peace and goodwill in the Church." Her references were sharp and clear, she was brilliant, and her delivery was in a beautiful voice with a British accent that Joe thought sounded like music.

After the meeting, when everyone stood up, most of the people were friendly. Several of the young ladies said hi, but the young brunette said nothing and walked to the door.

Joe walked out the front door and saw her standing there alone. Seeing no one there to greet her, he walked over to her. "I would be happy to walk you home."

She replied curtly, "Thank you, but I can do very well myself."

"I'm sure you can, but if you would do me the honor of letting me walk you home, I would be pleased."

She looked at him coolly. "Sir, I would be more comfortable and probably safer alone than in the company of a Yank. One of our generals said, 'The problem with the Yanks is they are overpaid, oversexed, and over here'. Some most unfortunate things have happened in this community. Thank you for your courtesy." She turned and walked away.

With dejection, he turned and walked down the street to see three American enlisted men approaching in his direction. As he readied his hand to return their salute, they cut diagonally across the street out of saluting range, and he heard one of them make some comment to the others about somebody being yellow.

Joe turned to walk back to the base and meditated. It wasn't easy. Yanks had misbehaved in a number of places, and there were too many of them here for the villagers to absorb. It was painful to be looked at as being yellow, but he really couldn't do anything about that. When his records caught up with him, it would probably help some. However, it didn't look like anything would change Armentrout's mind.

Strangely, he felt a sense of gratitude for his difficult childhood. Had he been glamorous and charming and a great athlete like Crole, this kind of thing would probably have just about put him under. But his memories of being the burned and somewhat stunted little kid with the big scars, of being the last one chosen when they chose up to play baseball, and of the arguments about which side would have to take him because nobody wanted to take him came back to him. He had survived this and his life had been rich. He found himself chuckling as he arrived back at the base because he had so little to bear.

Nearing his quarters, Joe could hear a booming, half-drunk voice. It was Sherman, the strongest and toughest of the pilots. He was a former professional boxer with an — I don't take nothing from nobody — attitude. He was okay sober but cut a wide swath when he was drunk.

Joe opened the door, stepped inside, and saw Sherman coming his way.

"Get out of my way, you yellow son of a bitch."

Sherman had never before been hostile. Joe made room for Sherman to pass, but the fighter came straight for him.

"Clear out of my way you yellow son of a bitch."

Joe took two hard jabs in the ribs and hit Sherman square on the jaw with a roundhouse right.

Sherman dazed and shaken, sobered up fast and worked Joe over with a professional flurry of lefts and rights.

Joe couldn't have lasted much longer when the others pulled them apart.

The next morning, when Joe and Sherman appeared before Col. Armentrout, Sherman looked great. Joe's black eye was barely visible due to makeshift camouflage from a mixture of shaving cream and talcum powder and his blood shot eye was screened with sunglasses.

Armentrout was curt. "Did you men fight last night?"

"Yes, sir," both answered.

"Who started it?"

"I did," snapped Sherman.

"It takes two to fight," Joe added.

"Who won?"

"I did," Sherman grinned.

"I expected as much. It takes courage to fight."

"Sir, I've been in the ring. I know yellow and I know courage. This man ain't yellow. He was beat but still coming at me when they stopped us. I've had years of training and experience. I doubt if Joe has ever fought before."

"We're in a war. In a war, you win or you lose. Excuses don't count."

"Oberlin, you didn't start it and you're being transferred. Nothing will be on your record."

"Sherman, you're a winner. We need winners. If you will coach boxing during PT, nothing will go on your record."

Sherman rubbed his jaw and grimaced. "I'll do it, sir. I'll coach Oberlin, too. He has the makings of a real fighter."

As they left headquarters, Joe sighed, "Thanks, Sherman."

"Bullshit. I don't know what makes you tick. I do know you weren't yellow last night. Armentrout has it in for you. I don't like to see a man hit when he is down."

C h a p t e r   I X
E n c h a n t m e n t

Sarah Bradford was sipping her morning coffee in her London flat when the phone rang.

"Hello, Mum."

"Hello, Ann. How are you? Why the morning call?"

"I need to talk."

"I'm flattered. Talk."

"Last night I was rude and mean."

"Are you sure? You never do that."

"I did."

"Tell me."

"A Yank pilot asked if he could walk me home after church, and I was rude to him."

"How?"

"He asked me nicely, and I told him no and quoted the trouble-with-Yanks bit. You know what the General said, 'The problem is the Yanks are overpaid, oversexed, and over here.'"

"Why did you do that?"

"At the time, I thought it was because of badly behaved Yanks hurting British girls including my good friend."

"Oh. Go on."

"Well, I'm not sure that was the reason."

"Tell me all about it."

"I was giving my views on the Apostle Paul's letters and his respect for women. The rest of the group didn't get my points, but the Yank did. He was keen, asked good questions, and was clearly open-minded. I'm sure he liked what he heard. His attitude thrilled me."

"Keep going. I need to hear more."

"He was nice looking. He seemed to be sensitive — none of that hotshot, cocky-pilot stuff.

"Mum, I don't know how to act around men. All the time I was growing up, I was such an aardvark. No boys ever looked at me."

"You were not an aardvark. You were a head taller than the other children, and you made such wonderful grades it intimidated your peers, but your teachers and all our family friends thought you were wonderful."

"It didn't bother me much then. I was lost in studies, secure at home, and had lots of confidence in myself."

"What happened last night? Did you suddenly discover that you are a beautiful young woman?"

"Not exactly."

"Then what?"

"Well, something I've not run into before. He has a really good mind and it excited me, but there was something else."

"Get to it, Ann. What else?"

"Well, you know I liked ballet, but I quit because I was tall and stood out from the other girls; and the boys didn't like to be pared with a girl who was taller than they were."

"What does that have to do with last night?"

"When that Yank walked up to me, he was three or four inches taller than I was. I felt something I've never felt before. I had those same feelings that I laughed at when my silly teen-age friends talked about them."

"Does it frighten you to be human?"

"It must have. I panicked and was rude."

"You had a right to be mad about what those Yanks did."

"Yes, but not at him. I'm sure he's not that kind."

Sarah Bradford's voice was gentle. "Ann, are you afraid of being a normal human being?"

"I don't think so. Why?"

"It sounds like last night you had very human feelings and they frightened you."

Ann's voice was thoughtful. "Tell me more."

"We have to remember that human beings are animals and have animal instincts and feelings. Your grandmother used to say that what sets good people apart from animals is that they control their animal instincts and feelings. That's what those bad Yanks didn't do."

"I didn't have that kind of bad feelings. It was a kind of thrill."

"I understand. Be happy. It's fun to be human. You'll handle it well. You have great discipline and strong beliefs. You just responded on the safe side. You'll probably get a chance to be kind to the Yank."

"Thanks, Mum."

"Thanks for calling. Don't write off that Yank. He sounds interesting and unusual."

C h a p t e r   X
B u g g e d   b y   t h e
B e e h i v e

While Joe was waiting for transfer, Crole prevailed on Col. Armentrout to let Joe fly a mission with his flight.

By luck, Joe was flying a plane that the ground crew called the Bee Hive because it had lots of bugs. The crew chief had it on the red diagonal, but Joe signed off on it and took it up.

The mission was routine with no action, but Joe noticed the oil pressure gauge begin to drop slowly. At first, he thought he would go ahead, but he remembered crashed planes and dead pilots don't win wars.

He radioed Crole. "Lost my oil pressure."

"Peel off and head home. You won't do us any good in a Kraut P.O.W. camp."

Joe peeled off and flew home. As he dropped to lower altitude, the oil pressure gauge began to rise. By the time he parked the Bee Hive the oil pressure was normal.

Joe told the crew chief what happened.

"Happened once before to a young lieutenant named Matthews. They racked his rump and shipped him out."

Joe went to de-briefings and then to his quarters. He felt sick at heart. All the talk about being yellow and now he would face charges. Maybe it would have been better if one of those Zeros had gotten him.

Ten minutes later, a first lieutenant appeared at his door.

"You are confined to quarters pending investigation for cowardice in aborting your mission without cause."

About an hour later, Crole showed up. "What happened? Armentrout's after your ass. Says the crew chief ran up that engine three times and the oil pressure was fine."

"I don't doubt it. It came back before I landed."

"Armentrout hates your guts, but he's a good officer. He busted Matthews for the same thing on the same plane, so I think there's a little question in his mind. He knows the ground crew believed Matthews."

"Crole, could I be crackin' up? I was sure that pressure dropped, but it came back before I landed. What bothers me is that a crazy person never thinks he's crazy, and I'm absolutely sure I lost my oil pressure. On top of that, I keep having that dream of a blinding flash, spiraling downward, and then absolutely nothing."

"Punt that one. I'd tell you flat-out if you were nuts. You aren't; in fact, you take crap better than anyone I know. Wait and see how this works out."

The next day, Evans the crew chief, Crole, and Joe received orders to report to Lt. Col. Armentrout's office.

Armentrout was angry. "Evans, did you check out the oil pressure on that plane after Captain Oberlin landed?"

"Yes, sir."

"How many times?"

"Three."

"How did it check out?"

"Fine all three times."

"Crole, did Oberlin beg off saying he'd lost his oil pressure?"

"He said he'd lost his oil pressure."

"This stinks! He has nothing to support it but a lot saying it isn't true!"

Crole spoke up. "May I speak, sir?"

"Yes."

"Evans, do you think Capt. Oberlin is telling the truth?"

"Yes, sir. I think Matthews was, too."

"Why?"

Evans looked at Crole. "Sir, should I tell the Colonel about last night?"

"Yes."

"Last night, Capt. Crole showed up with seven CO_2 fire extinguishers. He squirted that oil pressure gauge and the line back to the engine with a whole bottleful. The whole thing was white with frost when we revved up the engine."

"What happened?" snapped Armentrout.

"Nothing. The oil pressure was fine."

Crole was smiling slightly as he spoke. "Tell the Colonel what happened next."

"Capt. Crole just kept squirting that gauge line and the spot where it tied into the engine. He figured the first time didn't last long enough for the cold to soak in like it would at high altitude."

"What happened?"

"We revved the plane up and had no oil pressure. There's a cold bug in that system, sir."

Armentrout looked at Joe with a stone face. "You're off the hook on this one."

Then he turned to Crole. "I'll find Matthews and clear him."

As they walked back to quarters, Joe said to Crole, "You saved my hide, maybe more than that. You saved my peace of mind. I owe you."

"You owe me nothing. I'd have been booted out way back when if you hadn't saved my ass when I was drunk. You're not half as happy about this as I am. I love to make the brass back off. By the way, you did notice that even though Armentrout hates your guts he was fair, didn't you?"

"Yes, I noticed, but I'll be glad to get out from under him. He doesn't want to change his mind."

Chapter XI
Reconciliation
and Birth

The new squadron arrived at the base. It was under the command of a Colonel Chipman who carried the reputation of being a good and level-headed man. Joe was pleased when the new commander asked him to come over for an interview. Joe entered and saluted. He liked what he saw. He seemed to be all business.

Chipman spoke with an interested and comfortable manner. "I understand you've had some altercations with your squadron second in command."

"I wouldn't call them altercations, sir. It's just that he thinks people who don't drink, don't smoke, and don't chase women are yellow, and he believes I'm yellow."

"I understand it's not just your attitude toward smoking, drinking, and women, but when he told you off, you were not on duty and you just took it without giving him any kind of an answer."

"Sir, Colonel Armentrout was well into his cups. We were taught in Officer's Training never to deal with someone when he is drunk but to wait until he sobers up and then try to deal with him. I haven't had the chance since he sobered up. He is a very good officer. He enjoys an excellent reputation, but I sure put a burr under his saddle."

Chipman smiled. "Oberlin, tell me your history. What have you done since you got your wings?"

"Sir, if I tell you this, will you treat it as confidential? My records have not arrived. Until they do, if I started talking about it, people would think I was blowing smoke and it wouldn't help matters a bit. Those who don't agree with Armentrout wouldn't feel any different, and those who agree with him would think I'm not only yellow but a liar."

"You may proceed, I'll keep your confidence; now tell me about it."

"Sir, I was sent to the South Pacific. We had P-40s there. They're no match for the Zeros. We had a rough time with it. We did the best we could, but we didn't have good odds. I shot down four of them, but my records haven't caught up with me. If I talked about it now, it wouldn't have any credibility. I have to earn my own spurs here."

"I don't doubt you, Oberlin. Even Armentrout says you're the best shot on the base. Would you do me the honor of commanding my A Flight?"

"Yes, sir, I would be honored to. Thank you."

Joe enjoyed flying under Chipman and with the other officers. Chipman, realizing that Joe had more combat experience than he did, often asked Joe's counsel. Several times, he called him in to discuss the performance of the P-47 as compared to the P-40. Joe told him he thought the P-47 was a much better airplane. The P-47 might be a bit heavy and a bit clumsy, but it was well armored, tough, and fast enough. What concerned Joe was new pilots coming up against Germans who had been in air-to-air combat for years. Joe suggested that they had better do the same thing they did in the Southwest Pacific. He thought those German pilots would outmaneuver them if they tried to dogfight.

"You're probably right, Joe. We're going to find out. Next week we're going to start flying deeper over the continent. Are you ready for it?"

"Yes, sir, I am."

In the weeks that followed, Joe was credited with shooting down an ME 109 and a Nazi flag was painted on the side of his cockpit. Joe met Crole whenever he could in the Officer's Club, and they spent long hours talking. He told Crole about his experience in the South Pacific, and he swore him to secrecy because he didn't want the other pilots to think he was blowing smoke.

When Armentrout heard about Joe shooting down the ME 109, his only comment was, "He would have ratted out if there had been anything on his tail."

Joe couldn't understand Armentrout's attitude toward him. It was completely inconsistent with everything else he saw and heard about the man. The thought crossed Joe's mind that maybe Armentrout hadn't thought through the things he believed the way Joe had, and he found it uncomfortable to encounter a man who had strong personal convictions. He didn't know, and it was a sure thing that Armentrout didn't know and would probably never think about it. Maybe Armentrout's attitude protected him. Maybe he could shoot down an enemy plane and feel no pain for the other pilot. Joe couldn't do that.

Armentrout's mind bubbled with other things. He spent most of his spare time pursuing Maggie McQuire. Maggie was a delightful widow who was a captain in the Nursing Corps and head nurse at the base hospital. Joe heard that Armentrout spent a good many nights in her quarters.

Joe continued his distance running. Other officers who wanted to stay in shape and liked distance running more than calisthenics on the base joined him.

Whenever he could, he attended the discussion group at church on Sunday evening. The brunette was often there and sometimes almost friendly. Joe sensed that she noticed him but sensed even more that she had great distrust. He was somewhat reconciled to her attitude when he learned that one of the girls who had been attacked had been a friend of hers.

Joe loved the sound of her voice and noted that she moved with more grace than any woman he had ever seen. He suspected she had ballet training. At any rate, she wouldn't be around when winter came because she went to school at Cambridge. She was spending her summers here to help her grandfather with his farm.

#

On one unusually beautiful morning, Joe and several other pilots were out for a cross-country run. They knew they were not to fly until later in the afternoon and it was a great chance to work out. They were about a mile and a half from base, running past a pasture, when Joe looked over the stone fence and saw a cow straining to give birth to a calf. He recognized that the nose of the calf was protruding and had been for a long enough time that it was starting to swell. He knew that if something were not done promptly there would be a stillborn calf and probably a dead cow, too.

Joe snapped, "Something has to be done now." They trotted through the gateway of a country estate and up to a once magnificent country home. It was old and very rundown. The iron gate next to the road was off its hinge and several of the stone walls needed stones replaced. Joe went immediately to the backdoor and knocked. Much to his amazement, the black-haired, young lady came to the door.

Joe spoke softly. "Excuse me, but there is a cow in your pasture trying to give birth, and if something isn't done promptly, the calf will be stillborn, or both cow and calf will be dead."

She looked at him with concern. "We don't have any help right now. No one is here but my grandfather and he isn't strong enough to do it. The veterinarian has gone to the military service."

"Maybe I can help."

She looked at him solemnly. "If you can, we would appreciate it."

"Get some strong small ropes and one larger rope, and I will get the fellas to help me bring her into your barnyard."

Joe turned to his friends. "Come on guys, we are going to get the cow. You men get to play cowboy and midwife."

Then before leaving, he turned to the brunette. "If you can get a bowl of warm water and some soap, that would help, too."

The pilots thought it was great fun chasing the cow into the barnyard. Joe took the larger rope, put it around the cow's neck, and looped it around behind her front legs and in front of her rear legs in such a way that when you pulled the rope each loop would draw tight. He then turned to Crole. "Pull on the rope and she'll fall down."

"No way she'll fall down."

"Yeah, she'll fall down."

One of the other pilots piped up, "I'll bet you ten bucks she doesn't."

Crole showed his puckish grin. "I don't think she'll fall down either, but I'll bet ten bucks on Joe just because he's Joe."

Joe handed the rope to Crole. "Pull!"

Crole pulled it gently and nothing happened.

"Pull hard!"

Crole then gave it all he had and the cow's rear legs seemed to become paralyzed. She leaned to one side as the front legs weakened and she rolled on her side.

Crole grinned. "Ten bucks."

Joe heard an old man's voice bark, "By Jove, Ann, that young man knows what he's doing. What do you think he'll do next?"

Ann responded, "This is my grandfather, Brigadier Clarence Bradford. This is his farm and we both appreciate what you're doing."

Joe looked up. "How do you do, sir?" Looking at the old man with the great shock of bushy-white hair, which hung down over his ears, he saw the strong face of a military commander and the wrinkles of age. Joe liked what he saw.

Joe then washed his hands in the soapy water, reached down to the nose of the fetus, and pushed it back into its mother's womb. He then formed loops on the ends of the two smaller ropes, reached in the back of the cow, and hooked the loops above the hooves on each of the fetus's front feet. He pulled hard until one leg came out and then another leg came out. He turned around to the others and explained, "A cow can't get the legs, shoulders, and head all out at one time, but if you straighten out one leg and then the other leg and pull out and down, the whole fetus should come."

One of the pilots took one of the ropes and Joe took the other rope. They pulled very hard and a large fetus came out followed by a gush of afterbirth. Joe quickly wiped the nose of the fetus free of obstruction and pushed down on its chest several times until the calf was breathing on his own.

There was much muttering on the part of the other pilots, a loud, "Wow!" out of Crole, a happy, "Oh, wonderful," from Ann, and a booming, "Jolly good," from the Brigadier.

He pulled the ropes off the cow and shoved her a little with his foot. The cow started to get up. "Watch out, they can be killer-mean when they think they're going to protect their babies." However, the cow wasn't disposed to be mean. She seemed to sense that Joe was trying to help. She turned around and began to lick the calf vigorously.

"He'll stand up pretty soon. When he does, he'll have to nurse. Calves have to have the first milk from their mothers; it's called colostrum. If they don't get it, they don't make it. Watch closely; if you see his tail begin to shake, it means he's getting milk.

"We're going to have to get things gathered up and get out of here because we have to fly this afternoon."

As Joe washed in the soapy water, he looked at his running shorts, saw blood and afterbirth, and muttered to himself, "This is going to be hard to explain back at the base. But knowing these other characters, I won't have to." He looked at the other pilots. They were all agog. None of them had ever seen anything like this. They'd probably never seen anything born. They were a mixture of a little frightened at the sight of the blood and absolute amazement of the beginning of a life.

As they were starting to the gate, he heard Ann's excited voice say, "Oh, look, he's nursing."

Then he heard the booming voice of the old brigadier say, "By Jove, we'll name him Yank."

As they were trotting toward the base, the other pilots were lost in their thoughts. Crole came out of the quiet and looked at Joe with an impish smile. "When the talk of this gets around the club, they may still think you're square and dull, but they'll also know you can do things they never dreamed of. You'll probably get another nickname out of it. Probably something like Bloody Joe, but it won't be derogatory."

The next Sunday evening after the discussion at church, Ann Bradford was actually friendly. She came over to Joe. "The cow and calf are doing beautifully. The Brigadier suggested we name the calf Yank."

"Thank you. We appreciate the compliment. Now answer a question for me. Who is Sir Clarence? I met the Brigadier, but I heard people say you were related to Sir Clarence."

Ann laughed. "Oh, Joe, you're not familiar with things around here. Grandfather was knighted after the last war. The Brigadier and Sir Clarence are the same, but he likes to be called Brigadier, particularly around military people."

"I understand that when you come to these meetings on Sunday evening you spend the night with your aunt who lives down the street. Is the calf doing well enough that you would permit me to walk you to your aunt's?"

Ann looked at him solemnly and then smiled. "Yes, thank you. That would be lovely."

As they walked leisurely down the street, Joe asked, "What are you studying in Cambridge?"

"World history."

"I like history. I didn't like it in school, but I'm reading all the military history I can read now. We have a couple of West Pointers who have their textbooks. I've been reading about Caesar and about Napoleon. It's surprising the number of principles that are the same today as they were then."

"That's true of history in general. I don't believe you can really understand today or think about tomorrow if you don't understand where we came from."

Joe was thoughtful. "I believe you're right. History is fascinating. I don't quite understand the people who seem to think it's useless."

As they arrived at her aunt's door, Ann turned and smiled warmly. "Goodnight. See you next week at church."

Joe smiled back. "I'll be there if I'm not flying."

However, they were flying, and they were flying for the next three Sundays. A month after his chat with Ann, when he and the others were out on a cross-country jog, they noticed a P-47 diving and buzzing something.

Joe commented to Crole, "That idiot; it's against the rules. It makes the natives mad. He probably thinks he's having a lot of fun making cows run or something, but it really hurts our relations with everybody who lives here, and after all, this is their home."

Crole was philosophical. "We train them to be hot pilots then we get on them when they act like hot pilots, but you're right, somebody is going to have his butt in a sling."

A few minutes later, they saw a large black horse trotting toward them. The horse was holding its head high to keep from stepping on his reins and he was showing lather and fear. Joe looked, and then took another quick look and recognized the horse to be one he'd seen at the Brigadier's farm. Joe, seeing the empty saddle, felt sick in his stomach and ran out in front of the horse saying, "Whoa," gently and firmly and grabbing the reins. He vaulted into the saddle and rode headlong back up the country road. As he came over a hill, he saw a woman with long, dark hair sitting on the flat stones of the side of the bridge holding one leg and obviously in great pain. Joe rode up, dismounted, and walked up to see Ann sitting in a cold furry.

"You idiot Yanks."

"What happened?"

"I had stopped to pick some flowers. I was just mounting this horse when one of your airplanes came from nowhere and terrified him. He leapt and wheeled and threw me into the side of this bridge, and I heard something snap in my foot."

"We best get you to a doctor."

"There's no doctor in the village."

"This is a matter of our responsibility and we have doctors." Joe then picked her up and lifted her onto the horse. She barely had time to put an arm around his neck to stabilize herself and felt both great pain and thrill as his arms swept her from her perch to the horse.

Joe asked, "Can you sit the horse at a trot if I run ahead of you?"

She replied, "Well, I certainly can't post, but I'll endeavor to do it."

They had gone a very short distance when Crole and the other pilots came running up panting hard.

Joe snapped, "That idiot plane buzzed her and caused her serious injury. Could you run ahead and alert the hospital to be ready to deal with a broken foot and possible internal injuries caused by one of our pilots to a British citizen?" Then he said softly to Crole, "Tell them it's the Brigadier's granddaughter, and if they have any sense they'll roll out the carpet. Maybe you better tell them that, if they don't have any sense, they'll have the wrath of the Brigadier down their necks."

Before they arrived at the base, an ambulance met them and Ann was lifted onto a stretcher. As they left, Joe reassured Ann, "Don't worry about the Brigadier, I'll give him a ring." Then Joe tied the reins of the black horse over the saddle and tapped him on the rump knowing that frightened horses always run home.

When Joe called the Brigadier, the Brigadier, with military toughness that had been honed for years in the trenches of World War I, responded to Joe's report that the injuries were not life threatening with, "Good job, Captain. Thank you, be in touch."

The next morning Joe was up early. It was raining lightly and no flights were scheduled. Joe put on his slicker and went out to pick a bouquet of wild flowers, which he arranged in a tall tin can. He arrived at the hospital at 0800 and asked permission to see Ann. He looked a little bedraggled and weather-beaten as he came into her room bearing his tin can full of wild flowers.

Ann smiled warmly and said with candor, "This is the first time that I've ever had a man bring me flowers."

"How bad were your injuries?"

"One of the bones in my foot is broken, but they tell me it is in line and it's in a cast. They made a walking cast, so I can walk on it. I'll have to thump around for a few weeks, but they say everything will be lovely. They want me to stay another day to make sure I have no internal injuries, but they are treating me very well."

"I'm going to call the Brigadier to tell him how well you're doing. I'll tell him that that idiot who buzzed you and your horse is grounded under house arrest and awaiting court-martial. I think the Brigadier will appreciate the promptness. It was one of Armentrout's pilots. He's a West Pointer and a tough disciplinarian. I don't think this will happen again.

About twenty minutes later, Captain Maggie McQuire entered the room. It was clear to Joe that his presence was no longer acceptable. As the door closed behind him, Ann looked at Maggie. "Tell me about Capt. Oberlin. What do you know about him?"

Maggie's eyes twinkled, as she saw the earnestness of the question. "My girls know all there is to know about everybody on the base. The only negative that I know is that Colonel Armentrout thinks he's yellow. I don't think he's a coward. None of my girls thinks he's yellow, and I don't know a pilot who thinks he's yellow. He's already shot down two German airplanes, and he's the best shot in either squadron."

Ann frowned slightly. "That's not what I mean. Tell me about him."

Maggie smiled. "I thought there was more than an academic interest when you asked that question. I'll sum it up. If I were to pick any pilot in either squadron to marry my daughter, if I had a daughter, I would pick Joe. He's honest, he's fair, he's humble, he's square, and he's loyal. He might be considered rather dull because he doesn't enjoy drinking, smoking and whooping it up; and he's certainly no woman chaser. I suspect he's never had a serious girlfriend. In part because he's too shy, and in part because his friend, Crole, told me that his mother and Aunt Eve were phenomenal women. He has such a daunting yardstick, he's never found anybody."

Ann's eyes twinkled. "Anything you could do to shorten that yardstick would be appreciated. I can't measure up, but I'd sure like to try."

Chapter XII
Vindication

It was during the fourth game of chess and about the twentieth time that the Brigadier had referred to the Americans as Colonials that Joe was able to screw down his anxiety and rev up his courage to say, "Sir Clarence, why do you call us Americans Colonials?"

The Brigadier snapped back, "You Americans didn't win your independence; we jolly well gave it to you. We sent that idiot Burgoyne down from Canada. He was more interested in his mistress than he was in winning. Then he simply fizzled out and gave up and you people were given your first victory.

We won all the rest until that fool Cornwallis got himself bottled up in Yorktown and the French fleet got there ahead of ours. Cornwallis not only gave up, he didn't have the backbone to attend his own surrender ceremony. He played sick and sent somebody else. Then later, we reached an agreement with the French and swept you into it.

We gave you your independence. Half of our Parliament was on your side anyhow. We gave it to you by grace. But what I was saying — back in fifteen, sixteen, and seventeen when we were fighting the Germans — that was the real war."

Joe smiled. "Yes, sir, it was. You and men like you won it, and we are grateful. We're going to try and show you how grateful by winning this war."

The Brigadier knit his brow slightly. "Yes, but it's going to be a long pull."

When they finished the game and Joe started to leave, the Brigadier pushed his cane down in order to walk to the door with Joe, but he saw Ann enter the hall from a side room and sat back down, smiling, as he began to industriously put away the chess set.

When they were out of earshot from Sir Clarence, Ann almost whispered, "This farm is not doing well. I understand you have training in agriculture and know farming. Could you give me some help?"

"I'd be happy to do what I can."

"I'd like to have you look at the books some time."

"As soon as we have time, we'll study them."

He turned to go and heard Ann's voice say softly, "Joe?"

He turned back around, as Ann extended a hand holding a small white box tied with a ribbon. "The Brigadier and I wanted you to have this. We so appreciate all you have done for us and for taking time to play chess with him. I know you're in a hurry, but open it when you have time. We hope you'll enjoy it. You know it comes with sincerity from both of us."

Joe was pressed for time, as he hurried back to base. He changed into his flying outfit, but before going out the door, he quickly opened the package to find a beautiful white silk scarf with the Bradford crest embroidered in the corner. Joe had heard stories of pilots flying carrying the colors of people they cared about just as the knights of old had carried the colors of their ladyloves. He didn't want to read too much into it, but he grabbed the scarf and wrapped it around his neck as he ran out the door.

Two hours later on a mission over Belgium, they were escorting bombers when Messerschmidts appeared on the scene. Joe dove to fire on one, as a burst of anti-aircraft went off beside and slightly to the rear of the cockpit. It was a shuddering blow, as he felt the impact of shrapnel hitting him on the side of the head, face, and neck. The impact was hardest around the side of his forehead, and he could feel blood oozing into his eyes. He was grateful for the protective shield in the P-47; otherwise, he would be dead for sure. He grabbed his new scarf, wound it around his head, and tied it hard hoping to reduce the flow of the blood.

Joe called on the radio to his flight. "I'm hit pretty hard, bleeding a good bit, and think I'd better go home. You guys know the marching orders. Keep up the good work. I hope to see you back at the base."

The wind howled through the hole in the canopy, as Joe leaned forward to get as much protection as he could and put the P-47 in a climb trying to get altitude and coolness. He had heard cold reduces blood flow. If he hit any trouble on the way home, he'd need the altitude. At ten thousand feet, he was relieved to find his oxygen was still working.

It was then that he heard the call of Armentrout's voice. "I'm hit pretty hard. I'm headed home. I'm just north of Antwerp near the coast. I have limited control of my plane, and there are three Messerschmidts coming in on me. If there's anybody in the area, I need help."

Joe looked down, as he realized he was near the area and quickly caught site of a P-47 with Messerschmidts coming in behind him, one above and behind, and two lower and closer — one slightly ahead of the other. He slammed his throttle full ahead, climbed slightly, and dove straight to the rear-most Messerschmidt coming in very close because he wanted to get him before he could radio. He let fly with a burst. The plane burst into flame and rolled over. By the time it steered straight down, Joe was already firing at the second, which also rolled over. He saw a pilot bail out. Joe dove right on after the last one. As it banked to the right, Joe got a deflection shot off and the Messerschmidt flew right into it. Joe pursued him and used the last of his ammo. Then he said on his radio, "That takes care of them. I'll baby-sit you across the channel, but then I'm going to have to take off; I'm a bit under the weather."

Armentrout's voice boomed back, "That was great flying, great shooting. That last one just hit the drink. You saved my butt. Whoever you are, thanks a lot."

Joe snipped back, "We better go easy on the flattery, neither one of us is on the ground yet. Experienced pilots would not have been that easy to get."

"You sell yourself short, man, that was superb flying and gunnery."

Joe thought he had encountered a senior pilot coaching two rookies using a crippled American plane for target practice. In their fun, they had let their vigil down. There would be sadness in some German homes tonight. War was war, but gaining recognition for killing people ate at Joe's guts. If he thought about it too much, it would get to him.

By the time they reached the English coast, Joe was feeling light-headed and ill, so he gave it full throttle and radioed to the base that he was coming in wounded. He put his wheels and flaps down, made a smooth landing, taxied up to the waiting ambulances, cut his engine, and got a quick glimpse of the anxious look on the face of his crew chief and the assembled ground crew. As he pulled back the canopy, the crew chief was on the wing pulling hard with a look of almost horror as he saw the blood soaked scarf, the blood down the side of his head and all over his chest.

When the canopy came back, Joe pulled up but fell back in the seat. With the strong arms of the crew chief, he was able to move a little and was halfway out of the cockpit before he passed out. He slid through the arms of the crew chief who was barely able to hold his limp body, as it flattened out on the wing.

The medics ran forward and carefully slid the blood-sloppy, unconscious body onto a stretcher, which they threw in an ambulance. They roared off to the hospital. It was touch and go at the hospital. Plasma was started immediately. Joe's blood type was less common and only three men on the hospital record had the same type. In looking through their records, they noticed that Ann Bradford had the same type. Captain Maggie McQuire pointed out to the surgeon that the men from base were V.D. suspect; therefore, Ann Bradford would be the best option. A phone call brought Maggie the chosen donor with only one specification — no one must ever tell Joe.

His wounds were painful. They would leave ugly scars and had caused profuse bleeding, but they were not life threatening. It was the blood loss that was the big scare.

After Ann gave blood, she went out to see Maggie McQuire. "Maggie, was Joe wearing a scarf when they brought him in?"

"Yes. He was wearing a white scarf. He had it wrapped around his head twice and tied in a knot. As a matter-of-fact, it probably saved his life. It held the blood flow down enough to make it home. Without that scarf he would have never made it."

"What happened to the scarf?"

"It's over there with a bunch of stuff they cut off him. Do you want it?"

"Yes."

"You can sure have it."

She went over and picked it up. As she looked at all the blood-soaked garments, she felt a horrible cringe. "Maggie, could I stay with him tonight?"

"There will be nurses with him tonight. He's comatose. He'll be under heavy sedation and will be out of it for a day or so. He won't know anybody is here."

"But what if he takes a turn for the worse?"

"He has some good blood in him now and plasma. The only thing we have to worry about is infection and figure out how to feed him the way he's sewed up."

"If I come back early in the morning, may I sit with him?"

"Yes, that's probably better medicine when he wakes up than anything we can do for him."

#

Joe's first feelings were like a man coming out of deep water following a dive and seeing the surface above him. He felt himself rising toward light until he realized that he was Joe and he was alive. Oh, what a headache. And what's holding my hand? What's touching my hand? His head hurt intensely, but he forced one eye open slightly. It was what he felt like it was. His hand, hanging down at the side of the bed, was being pressed against a lady's cheek. He could see the black hair he loved so much. He slowly turned his head back and decided this was too good to waste; I won't let anybody know I'm awake.

He lay there for about an hour until he heard the door open and felt the cheek quickly pulled from his hand. He heard a doctor's voice saying, "How are you, Joe? Can you feel anything? Can you hear me? If you can hear me, wiggle your fingers."

Joe was a little afraid that his ruse might be known if he responded too quickly, so he held still until the doctor reached down, touched his other hand, and squeezed it. He squeezed back. Then he tried to talk and realized he couldn't. His jaw was bound.

The doctor was grave. "Joe, if you're feeling pain, squeeze my hand. We can give you something for it."

Joe squeezed his hand.

"Joe, you're going to be all right. You have a lot of stitches in you; you'll have some scars, but most of them will be covered up with hair. I think the others won't be noticeable in a year or so. If they are, we can do surgery and make them less noticeable, but you have to prepare yourself for a few things.

"One of them is that you're going to recover completely, and you'll be back flying in six weeks to a couple of months.

"Number two is when we take these bandages off; you're going to look awful. Don't let it scare you. It isn't permanent, but it isn't going to do your ego any good when you see yourself. We had to shave about half of your head. You're going to be swollen and you're going to be sore. You're going to be red and you're going to be ugly, but the scars won't be bad and they won't be permanent. As a matter-of-fact, when your hair grows out, any scars left will be just enough to be fashionably glamorous.

"Now get that through your head. Don't waste a lot of time on one of these big ego-pity parties when you see yourself. Will you do that for me? If you will, squeeze my hand."

Joe squeezed his hand, and then turned his head to Ann who was holding the other hand and squeezed it.

Two days later, a much-bandaged Joe Oberlin was sucking a milkshake through a straw. He was too bandaged and stitched to chew.

The door opened and Col. Armentrout walked in. Armentrout looked like he had been drug through a knothole backwards. He was not really shaking, but he was shaken to the core. He looked at the bandaged man in front of him. "Oberlin, did you know that was me who called for help?"

Joe nodded his bandaged head up and down.

"Did you know I had called you everything in the book including a yellow son of a bitch?"

Joe nodded his head up and down.

Armentrout looked at him. "Then why in the hell did you save my ass?"

Joe reached to the side of the bed, picked up a little pad of paper and wrote:

Do unto others, as you would have them do unto you.

Recompense no man evil for evil.

You're one of the best, if not the best, officers in the Army Air Force. You're the best officer we have, and if we're going to win this war, we can't lose you.

He pulled the paper off the pad and handed it to Armentrout.

Armentrout took the paper, read the first line and wiggled his nose up a little, read the second line and curled his lip as if to snarl, and read the third line.

"Well, I'll be damned. Did you really know what my attitude toward you was?"

Joe nodded his head, and then with his right hand, palm up, stuck his middle finger straight up in the air and gave him the finger. Armentrout burst out laughing. "You got that one right. I have to go now."

Joe whipped up a smart salute to Armentrout, and then, as he held the salute waiting for Armentrout to return it, dropped all the fingers except the middle finger that remained a sharp salute.

Returning Joe's salute, Armentrout looked him square in the eye and then dropped all the fingers except the middle one, turned around, and walked out the door. As he walked down the hall, he shouted, "Where the hell is Captain McQuire?"

Chapter XIII
Home Town

Charlie Hicks mumbled to himself, as he drove down the gravel road to the Oberlin farm.

"Wish I'd never been a telegrapher. Wish I'd let Zeb deliver this. I had to do it for Chris and Mary."

As he banged the brass knocker on the old farmhouse door, he looked at the blue-star service flag hanging in the window and mumbled to himself, "At least it's not gold yet."

The door opened and he watched Mary Oberlin's warm smile dissolve in anxiety as he handed her the yellow envelope.

"Is he . . . ?" Mary choked.

"He's alive."

"How bad?"

"Don't know. You'd better read it. I'll go out back and find Chris."

Chris Oberlin came through the back door on the run, read the telegram twice, and embraced Mary.

Charlie spoke softly. "I'll go get Ed."

Both voices rasped, "Thanks, Charlie."

Mary let go of Chris, cranked the telephone, and picked up the receiver.

"Central?"

"Yes."

"Oh good, it's you. Please start the prayer chain. Joe's been wounded in action. We don't know how badly."

Tears dripped from Mrs. Osgood's eyes, as she called the first people on the Methodist Church prayer chain. As the senior telephone operator, she knew the town better than anyone. Without hesitation, she also called the Catholics, the United

Brethren, the Presbyterians, and the Pentecostals knowing that each individual would call the next to ask for prayers for Joe.

Ed Riley's car skidded to a stop in the Oberlin driveway. He hobbled rapidly into the house and read the telegram. "The odds are he'll make it. It says he was wounded in action. That means he was probably hit over the continent and he was able to make it back. Let's keep our chins up. Have you called Annie?"

"No, we don't know what to do. It's exam time at I.U. Should we wait till we know more?" asked Mary.

Chris Oberlin was firm. "Call her. Tell her Ed says it looks good. It wouldn't be fair to leave her out."

The telephone rang a series of long rings. Ed flinched. "That's the general ring. There must be a fire."

Chris picked up the receiver, listened, and then hung up.

"Mrs. Osgood wanted to make sure all our neighbors knew, so she called the general ring on the party line."

Mary took a deep breath. "Fresh air would help. Let's walk a little."

As they walked across the front yard, Ed pointed across the fields toward a neighbor's buildings. "Look at that. That barefoot kid is running as fast as he can to tell the neighbors who don't have phones."

Mary sobbed, swallowed, and gasped, "And Joe always felt people around here didn't think much of him. We have to go back in now. I am ready to call Annie, and then we'll pray."

Mary hung up the phone. "Annie took it better than I feared. She asked some questions and then said firmly, 'He'll be fine. I will not believe anything else.' I didn't argue with her. I just pray she's right."

Their prayers and meditation halted abruptly as the noise of cars coming into the drive made meditation impossible.

The first car held the Methodist and Presbyterian ministers with their wives and the Catholic priest. Riding on the running board, holding onto the car's doorframe, was the trash collector, Norman Stump. Norman was in his late twenties. He hadn't been able to get past the third grade. He was loud, but he was kind.

As the others moved toward the house, Norm turned to the other arrivals and almost shouted, "It ain't fair. It ain't right. He's been shot twice already and it ain't fair nor right."

As the clergy entered the house, their wives hugged Ed and Chris and embraced Mary. The protestant ministers were silent, but Father O'Malley spoke up with his Irish accent. "Norm's right. It's not fair or right; that's why we're here. The other clergy weren't home or they'd be here, too. Let us pray."

When the clergy left, Chris sighed. "I have to do chores. It will do me good to sweat."

As he started for the barn, he saw men repairing the barnyard fence. When he entered the barn, the cow had been milked and all the animals fed. One of the neighbors looked at him sympathetically. "You better go back in the house and tell Ed his chores are done, too."

Chris went into the house, spoke to Ed, and returned to the barn.

"All of you will have to stay for supper. There's more food in the kitchen and dining room than we could eat in months. I suspect, since it got here so fast, a lot of it was to be your suppers. Anyway, we'd like your company. It's a tough day."

That evening, a steady flow of hurrying new arrivals promptly went to Chris, Mary, and Ed then dissolved into the others in the kitchen, dining room, yard, and barnyard.

Later, Dr. Edwards arrived. He was a World War I surgeon who had been decorated for bravery for continuing to operate while shells ripped through the hospital. With no visible emotion, he spoke to Mary, Chris, and Ed. "Most of my wounded made it and we didn't have what doctors have now. If he has burns, the concern is sepsis."

"What's sepsis?"

"Infection."

Ed spoke quickly, "I doubt if he has burns. If his plane were burning, he wouldn't have made it back. It has to be shrapnel or bullet wounds."

"If he survived that long after impact, his chances are pretty good. Blood loss would be the risk, but they have plasma and can do transfusions. Remember, Joe is tough. As a child, he handled his burns well. Each day with no news means the odds are better."

That evening, Ted Hansen, editor of the weekly paper, was eating a sandwich in the local restaurant when Dr. Edwards walked in.

"Paper gone to bed, Ted?"

"Yes."

"Front page?"

"All Joe."

"You look tired. I'll bet you had to rewrite the whole thing."

"Sure did. Funny thing, I'm supposed to be putting out news, but everyone already knows about Joe. I've been sitting here wondering if I rewrote the front page because I wanted to or because folks would have my hide if I didn't."

Dr. Edwards beamed one of his rare smiles. "You wanted to. That struggling little lad got under your skin just like he did mine. Those church folks are praying up a storm. That will help them and could well help Joe, but, Ted, with you and me it's different."

"How so, Doc?"

"We think the good Lord can handle things without our instructions."

"You know, Doc, they laugh about us country folks as hicks, but we live better and Joe knows it. When he was home on leave, he told me an interesting story."

"What was it, Ted?"

"He said that when he was stationed at a training base in some little town in Colorado he called home and had to go through the Denver operator. The Denver operator heard our operator ring his home number, but there was no answer. Instead of our operator saying there was no answer she said, 'Hold on. I saw them drive north. I'll run them down,' and she did. Joe said he could hear that Denver operator laughing and telling the other operators while he waited, but our operator found his folks. He said, 'Let them laugh, we live better.' I agree with Joe."

"You're right. Do you think our people know it?"

"In their heads most don't, but in their guts they do."

#

Things eased a little each day. On the eighth day, a letter arrived from Crole.

Dear Mr. and Mrs. Oberlin and Mr. Riley,

Joe is going to be okay. The doctors say he will be back flying in two months.

Right now, he looks awful. His wounds are from shrapnel. They are all on the side of his head. He can't move his jaw and his face is all red and purple. He is healing well. His hair will cover most of the scars. They say there will be very little to see in six months.

Don't worry about the lucky stiff. The nurses are very attentive, and a beautiful British girl is there every day. She reads a lot of history to him. She is one smart woman. She stimulates his thinking and challenges his thoughts.

Don't worry — be happy — Joe is.

Thanks for raising the best friend I ever had.

Sincerely,

Crole

P.S. When he was all shot up, he shot down three Kraut planes on the way home.

Chapter XIV
Recuperation

Col. Armentrout, now commander of his squadron and sporting eagles on each shoulder, looked at Captain Crole. "Crole, you're his best friend. Do you think Oberlin would take the position as my deputy? And will you be p.o.'d because you feel passed over?"

Crole looked at Armentrout. "What makes you think he'll take it? You pooped all over him."

"I can't figure why I was so sure he was yellow. I think it was because my dad told me that during WWI he lost some good men because a guy who didn't smoke, drink, or womanize was yellow in battle. When Joe and I were off duty, I told him off. He didn't come back at me, so I figured he was yellow, too.

"You think he'll take it?"

"Yeah, I think he'll do it."

"Why?"

"'Cause he's no grudge holder. He has every right to hate my guts and he's my best friend."

"How's that?"

"We started out as the worst of enemies. He and I had nothing in common. You know, Armentrout, sir, you and I are officers and gentlemen because the Act of Congress says we're officers and gentlemen. He's an officer and he's a gentleman because that's the way he is. He may be dull as hell sometimes and his squareness may wear thin, but the guy has a good head, a real good head. He has guts and he has horse sense. He is one patriotic son of a bitch."

Armentrout grinned and scratched his head. "That's about the most left-handed endorsement I ever heard. If I ask him, are you going to feel passed over and honked off?"

"No, he's the only man in the army I'd rather serve under than you."

Armentrout grinned. "Hoped you'd take it that way. I put you in for major and I'm going to put him in for major. He'd be a major now if I hadn't screwed him. He'll be laid up for two months. He'll be a major before he gets back and he'll be a lieutenant colonel as fast as we can do it."

Crole grinned. "Armentrout, sir, you're a good officer, but you're hard to read. Thank God you don't carry a grudge when you know you're whipped."

Armentrout looked at Crole. "Did you know he shot down four Jap planes before he ever got here?"

"Yes, sir."

"Why didn't you tell me?"

"He asked me not to tell anybody, so I didn't. Joe isn't proud of it. He hates the thought of killing people. You or I would be proud as hell of a record like his, but his only pride is that he did his duty for his country, and he kept a bunch of our guys from being killed. It worries him so much I worry about him."

"The paperwork came through on that man today. Did you know that he had two Purple Hearts?"

"Yes, sir."

"Did you know that he also had the Air Medal?"

"Yes, sir."

"Did you know he had the Distinguished Flying Cross, the Bronze Star, and the Silver Star?"

"No. I knew he'd been put in for some stuff, but I didn't know it came through."

"At the time I was calling him yellow, he had the best combat record on the base. He spent the whole time fighting off a yellow-charge initiated by me."

"Like I told you, he doesn't carry a grudge. He doesn't even know he has most of those medals. When he does, I'll tell you what his reaction will be. He'll be embarrassed. He won't talk about it. He'll try to get out of having any presentation ceremony. Armentrout, sir, you are one very lucky officer."

"How's that, Crole?"

"Cube always thought you were a good officer even when you were dumping on him. He reads people with uncanny skill. I suspect he learned it working with animals or maybe he was born with it, but whatever, it probably saved your rear."

"I don't get what you're saying, Crole."

"Remember Colonel Botts?"

"Wasn't he the C.O. at a basic training field who went bonkers?"

"Yeah, he was the C.O. when Cube and I went through basic. He was cruel and sadistic. He didn't bother us much because we were officers, but he delighted in ruining cadets."

"Go on, Crole. I want to get what you're saying."

"It really bugged Joe to see those cadets abused. Being tough was okay, but this guy Botts was too much. He decided he wanted a nice green lawn on the slope in front of his headquarters; so, he told his TAC officers to gig the cadets until they racked up enough discipline tours to make and seed the lawn."

"Tours were supposed to be walked in dress uniform."

"Not to Botts. He got his green lawn okay. As a matter of fact, he felt great about it because so many people came to look and seemed so happy. The spirit of the whole base picked up when the grass came up. Col. Botts would always park in back then go to his office and watch the joy on the faces that looked at his sloping lawn. Then one day he went out the front door himself to look at it."

"So?"

"The grass was starting nicely, but coming up in the grass were lines of vigorous lettuce and radishes that you could read a block away."

"What did they say?"

"Base Cesspool."

Armentrout burst out laughing.

"Then what?"

"Botts realized that all that happiness was really laughing at him and he cracked up. That probably saved a lot of good pilots from being washed out and headed off a bunch of court-martials."

"Did Joe do it?"

"I never asked him. I didn't want to know in case there was an inquiry. You decide for yourself. I saw him in a garden store the week the lawn was planted, and he was the only guy in basic who had studied agriculture."

"You know, Crole, I'm beginning to understand what you see in him."

"Now you see why I say you're lucky. He thought you were a good officer entitled to your own opinions."

"Any man who will fly and fight like he did when he's wounded to save somebody ought to get the Medal of Honor. I was a real horse's ass, yet he almost cashed in to save my hide."

Crole looked at Armentrout. "You know, you couldn't kill him off with shame, now you're going to try and kill him off with embarrassment. Are you just trying to clear your conscience?"

"I thought about that. I wonder if he'll think that I'm asking him to be my deputy out of conscience."

"Put it to him straight and he'll deal with it, but if you're putting him in for the big casino because of your conscience, don't. Play it straight. Armentrout, sir, beneath all the crap, you're a good man."

#

A week after being sewed up, Joe could now open his mouth wide enough to insert small bites of food and was able to talk softly, so if you listened closely, you could understand what he was saying.

Captain Maggie McQuire entered his room followed by Ann and Brigadier Bradford. Captain McQuire handed him a sheet of orders. He quickly looked at the signature and saw Col. Chipman's signature:

> *To: Captain Joseph Oberlin*
> *From: Colonel George Chipman — Commanding*
> *Captain Joseph Oberlin, you are hereby ordered to proceed in the company of Miss Ann Bradford and Brigadier Bradford to Bradford Hall, thereto, to reside for four weeks under the supervision of the Brigadier and Miss Bradford.*
> *You are to report weekly to base hospital, United States Army Air Corps Base, North Chevington. You are to report immediately any change in your health to said hospital. Twenty-eight days from today, you are to report in my office along with your medical records to determine what service you may render subsequent to that day.*

Joe read over the orders and looked at the Brigadier who had a whimsical smile to his face. Joe sensed he was savoring a few games of chess. He looked at Ann who had an expression of total disinterest and duty. As he looked at Ann, he again marveled at that woman. He was absolutely sure that she and Maggie McQuire had connived and flimflammed the whole thing. Yet to look at her you'd think she was downtown in some city waiting on her bus.

A few days before he was to leave Bradford Hall, Ann asked him to look over the books of the farm. She had gone through, organized, and summarized the annual inventories and the annual sales of livestock.

Joe looked at them. "There is something badly wrong here. It seems to me that you're getting half or less than half of what you're producing and the rest is going somewhere else. Furthermore, your costs are too high. I think you're getting beat out on both ends of the line. Who would you suspect?"

Ann pondered. "We have lots of helpers who come and go. No one seems to stay very long.

"Grandfather has total faith in Barkley, the manager. He won't listen to any questions. Frankly, I'm not comfortable around him. Grandfather defends him always referring to brothers in combat. During the Great War, Barkley was his batman.

"Grandfather has really paid little attention to the farm. He isn't well enough to get around. He likes the horses. The tally on the horses seems to work out just about right while everything else is out of kilter."

"Ann, let's saddle up and ride over the whole farm. The place seems to be terribly run down, but with this kind of income it would have to be."

"Grandfather keeps it going by using part of his pension and the income from investments he has. But they are slipping, and if we can't turn it around, I'm afraid he'll be in real trouble as he gets older."

As they rode from field to field, Joe saw excellent pastureland badly neglected with shrubs and bushes growing in fields that should have been mowed. The stone fences seemed to be in reasonably good repair. Joe made a point of watching all the perimeter fences to find places where animals could have escaped and looked for skeletons, bones, or other debris left from predators. They found little evidence of predators. The fences were fundamentally intact all around the outside of the fifteen hundred acres.

Once back in the house, he put in a call at the base for a crew chief named Naranjo. Sergeant Naranjo was a chief in the Navaho tribe who had grown up on the reservation. Joe had talked with him about tracking when he was on standby waiting to fly. He arranged for Sergeant Naranjo to come to the farm when he had a few hours off.

He and Ann went to talk with the Methodist minister who knew everybody in town. After getting his pledge for complete secrecy, they asked about the supplier of gasoline and the supplier of feed and found they could be talked to in confidence.

The supplier of gasoline was clearly of the opinion that the Brigadier understood that each time he filled the tank at Bradford Hall he also filled the tank at Barkley's farm. Barkley had told him that this was part of the arrangement and that he used the gasoline for the work of the Brigadier. They asked if he would mind recording how much he had delivered to each place each year and that he keep this completely confidential. He agreed to do both.

When they went to the feed supplier, they learned nothing other than it had all been delivered to Bradford Hall and had verified his records were in agreement with the records of Bradford Hall. Joe suggested to Ann that they watch closely when Barkley came and went to see if he might be removing feed.

The next morning when Barkley drove in, he looked over things in general, directed the most recent worker to do some things, and then drove on back and parked next to the feed storage.

Joe and Ann walked out, obviously taking a walk in the opposite direction, walked around Bradford Hall, and found a spot in a wooded area where they could observe. As they chatted and watched, they saw Barkley lift the lid on the boot of his car and place several feed sacks in it then put the lid down again. Barkley made no effort to drive away, just went on doing his business. Careful observation showed that Barkley did this daily.

When Naranjo arrived, they explained the animal disappearance to him indicating that they had nothing current, but they would like his observations on what might be going on. Naranjo, with his usual calm face, responded with enthusiasm. He hadn't had a chance to do any tracking for a long time and even a cold trail was exciting.

They walked the perimeter of the farm and when they reached the far corner Naranjo stopped, jumped the fence, walked back and forth on down to a small stream, and then searched the brush.

They watched him, impressed with his thoroughness and the number of times that he bent down to examine things closely. They anxiously awaited his comments. As he came over the fence, he didn't immediately walk up to them but walked back and forth examining the rocks on the inside as he had on the outside.

Then he turned to them. "This is where they went. These rocks, unlike the others, have been taken down and put up frequently for a long time." He showed the lichens on them and the scratches on the lichens of the corner rocks. Then he led them farther away to see the unscratched lichens. Naranjo was confident. "Animals have passed over on the other side close together. In the bushes by the stream, there are gates that have been used to corner and pressure animals." He walked out in the field away from the corner of the stone fence. On a couple of occasions, he stopped and flicked in the ground with his knife.

He called to them, "Stakes have been driven in here. They have made a crowd pen in the corner and forced animals over the wall. When it's partially taken down, the sheep can easily jump it. They might even have used Judas goats to lead them."

The farm on the other side of this corner belonged to a man named Condon. Ann recalled that her grandfather said he didn't know much about him, but he was a cousin of Barkley's who bought the place about twenty years ago.

Ann looked at Joe. "What does it mean?"

"I don't know for sure, but it looks to me like they've been stealing your grandfather's sheep for a long time."

"What are we going to do?"

"We must catch them and get as much of your grandfather's money for him as we can. If he doesn't get it squared away, he's going to go under. It's about time to wean this year's lambs. I understand that's when they go back into this pasture. We better lay our plans quickly."

Sergeant Naranjo looked around with a faint grin. "If we can catch them, I can put an Indian scare into them and get a confession."

Joe smiled. "We might have to do that Sergeant. We'll work out a plan and be back in touch with you. You have any recommendations?"

"Yeah, catch him in the act. They talk better if you catch them in the act."

That night, Ann called her father in London and explained to him all of the things they had learned.

About an hour later, he called back. "A man named Peters, who is a senior operative for Scotland Yard and a personal friend, is currently on recuperative leave from a gunshot wound. He is feeling pretty good and is quite bored. He heard the story and would like to have a restful, recovering visit at Bradford Hall. He will be there tomorrow."

It was a very delicate situation. The old Brigadier was a wonderful man and one of the things that made him great was his fanatic loyalty to people he had served with. There was no point in talking with him until they had Barkley cold.

When Peters arrived, he was an engaging individual, obviously intrigued with the idea of looking into sheep stealing having always dealt with very complex crimes in the big city. Peters was pleased to get acquainted with Joe saying that his agricultural experience would be very helpful. He hoped to meet Sergeant Naranjo because he had heard that the American Indians were great in observing clues and tracking. Peters was not what one would expect for a senior agent in Scotland Yard. He was a roly-poly, red-haired fellow with a great grin and a bounce to his walk.

Joe was excited. "You know, sir, we Americans are in kind of a loose situation over here in not being citizens. We have some very talented people, Sergeant Naranjo being one of them. If you needed some unconventional assistance, we could render it. In addition to that, we can be kind of frightening when we land and take off if it's of any utility."

Peters grinned. "This is going to be the most smashing vacation I've ever had, particularly since I'm being paid on recovery leave while I'm here. Do you have any suggestions?"

"It occurred to me a confession might be hard to come by. This man Condon probably is the weak link. If we could catch him red-handed, it might be very helpful in breaking the whole thing wide open. If Condon turns out to be weak, Naranjo might be able to get a fast confession."

Peters grinned again. "That would be jolly good fun to see. If we had witnesses, his confession would hold up in court."

Peters thought a little. "If this has been going on this long, there's a chance that Barkley has an in with the local officials. It will be very useful to get our help from you people. Do you fly at night?"

"No, not now. I suspect we will before too long. I'll leave you phone numbers. If you see something going on, I will be here with Naranjo."

"Thanks. I agree that the best thing to do is to catch them in the act, and then roll this thing up from there."

Five days later, an orderly woke Joe. "A message was phoned in. Peters needs you."

Joe jumped up, dressed rapidly, and ran to the enlisted men's barracks, shook Sergeant Naranjo. "We better hurry."

Naranjo dressed quickly. "I have to stop by the hospital. Would you get a bottle of ketchup? I'll meet you at the gate."

Joe grinned. "I don't know what's up, but it sounds good to me. See you at the gate."

Joe arrived at the gate in a jeep. Naranjo jumped in with a little package in his hand, and they went as rapidly as they could toward Bradford Hall, turning their lights out and driving by moonlight as they came near so they wouldn't alert anyone. Ann and Peters met them. Joe opened his mouth, but Ann pre-empted him.

"I am going, too. You'll need a witness, and he is my grandfather."

Joe recognized a stone wall when he saw one and nodded. "Okay."

Sergeant Naranjo's excitement gleamed in his eyes. He reminded Joe of a cat pursuing a mouse. His every movement was supple yet tense. He was clearly on the hunt. No exchange of words was necessary. Naranjo was going to lead this expedition and the rest would follow.

They kept behind him, following his hand instructions, and arrived concealed at the corner of the farm to see sheep being driven over the fence. When about one hundred fifty sheep had passed over the wall, the thieves stopped. They drove them up to Condon's buildings and penned them. Then the two men walked into a shed, apparently, to enjoy a nip out of a bottle and a smoke.

Joe, Peters, and Naranjo walked through the door with drawn guns. Peters commanded, "Silence!"

The reaction of Condon was one of fear, but his somewhat obese, not very bright-looking assistant, showed abject panic. Naranjo grabbed the assistant, took him outside the shed, and growled, "You talk." Unbeknown to either Peters or Joe, Naranjo had put black and white stripes down each side of his face. He looked frightful.

As they held Condon at gunpoint, they heard two blood-curdling screams from outside the shed. Shortly, Naranjo reappeared, looked at the threesome, and spoke with an accent Joe had never heard. "Him talk. Me teach to talk."

Peters stared at Condon. "Are you ready to sign a confession explaining how long you have been stealing and how many sheep you have stolen from the Brigadier over the years?"

Condon was obviously terrified but not ready to move. Both Joe and Peters looked at Naranjo.

Naranjo glared at Condon. "This man talk."

He lifted up a large, vicious-looking knife dripping with bright red slime. They quickly turned their flashlights on the knife and then back on Condon's face and saw him blanch.

Then Naranjo growled, "Maybe I take more from this one," and held out his hand that contained part of a human ear and a finger all gushed in red slime.

Joe felt his stomach retch. That ear and finger were real. Naranjo moved them to show they were truly human parts. Was Naranjo going berserk?

Condon began to babble, "I'll talk. I'll talk. I'll tell you everything. I'll put it in writing. I'll sign it."

Ann listened intently as Peters interrogated and Condon babbled on and on. Peters put it in the form he wanted it. Ann wrote it all down and Condon signed it.

Peters spoke calmly, "From the figures you've given me, your share of this equals approximately the value of your farm. Are you ready to sign over and deed your farm to the Brigadier?"

Condon whimpered, "Yes, yes, anything, anything, I'm at your mercy."

A few minutes later, the constable arrived to take Condon and his assistant into custody. Joe was anxious and somewhat perplexed when the terrified assistant arrived pale but with no wounds.

Both Peters and Joe looked at Naranjo as they led off the assistant. "What did you do?"

Naranjo, having dropped his 'Injun' accent, responded, "All I had to do was tell him that, if he didn't want to get hurt, he had to show me the best and most terrified scream he had. I thought he did rather well. You probably wondered why I had to stop by the medical facility. I'd arranged with the sergeant in charge there to borrow a few spare parts from the last crash. I will wash them up and get them back, but I thought they did the job well."

Peters was jubilant. "Magnificent, old boy, magnificent."

#

Joe and Ann entered the Brigadier's study accompanied by Peters who spoke. "Splendid news, sir. We have apprehended the thieves and will restore your losses."

"Good show. Who were the culprits?"

"A man named Barkley was the leader aided by his cousin and a henchman."

The Brigadier's jaw went slack as he spoke softly, "Not my Barkley?"

"Afraid so, sir."

The Brigadier jerked himself upright and barked, "Treason! Prosecute to the fullest."

A few days after Barkley was incarcerated and confronted with all the hard evidence, he confessed. Restitution was ordered and the Brigadier's finances were restored.

Ann located a couple of young, disabled vets who were looking for jobs. Within weeks, Bradford hall was reviving.

When Peters left, he appeared like a boy who had been to the circus. He was happy to have helped his good friend's father, he enjoyed meeting Joe and the other Americans, and he was fascinated with Naranjo.

"Jolly good time with the lot of you. Would like to have that Naranjo at Scotland Yard. Seems to me we can do a good job with you Yanks in a lot more ways than just fighting the Jerrys. Good to meet you." He then turned and went bouncing away toward his car for his trip to London.

During Joe's stay at Bradford Hall, Ann followed the instructions to gently work a salve onto the healing wounds on Joe's head, scalp, temple, and jaw. She did this morning and evening with an empathetic touch after which Joe often would go to the mirror, sometimes saying, "I look like a Frankenstein monster."

Interestingly enough, the Brigadier had great admiration for the wounds. "Major, you now look like a soldier, like a real soldier — one who's been there and who's done it. I'm proud of you boy, proud of you."

One afternoon, Joe and Ann were walking over the farm observing the progress and enjoying the lush British countryside when Ann almost whispered. "I have a confession to make."

"What's that?"

"That first night at church when we walked out, you asked if you could walk me home, and I was rude to you. I didn't quite tell you the truth. I said some unkind things about Yankee soldiers.

They were true, but that wasn't the real reason. The real reason was that you were so handsome it made something skip inside me. I was afraid of myself and maybe a little afraid of you. You were so handsome."

Joe snorted, "I was so handsome, and now I look like a monster. You mean all this is sympathy for an ugly man?"

Ann was shocked. "Don't be stupid."

"What do you mean, don't be stupid? I'm not stupid. I look at the mirror and I see. I look God-awful ugly."

"Joe, you look handsome."

"Don't lie to me. I look ugly. I know what I look like, I've seen it." Joe's blood pressure was rising, but so was Ann's.

"Do you think everything has to look like something out of your Hollywood to be beautiful?"

"Ugly is ugly, beauty is beauty, handsome is handsome, and I'm flat-out ugly. I know it, you know it, so don't try to lie to me about it."

"Don't call me a liar."

"Don't try to lie to me."

As the argument grew more intense, they turned and walked back to the house. As they walked through the door, they were shouting. Joe was red-faced. "It's bad enough to be ugly as sin but being lied to about it is intolerable." He turned to stalk off when he ran head-on into the Brigadier.

For the first time, Joe heard the Brigadier's command voice. A thunderous voice barked out, "What's going on here?"

"I know I'm ugly as sin with all these wounds. I don't like to be lied to about it, and your granddaughter is lying to me."

Ann's voice was shrill. "This idiot has no comprehension that wounds earned in a noble cause can be beautiful. He has no sense of real beauty."

The Brigadier looked at Ann and bellowed, "I don't either." He reached up and pulled a shock of white hair from his head, showing the top of the right ear burned off with horrible scarring. Half of his scalp showed curly ugly scars.

He looked at Joe. "White phosphorus in the trenches, you know. Damnable stuff. Those bloody Krauts used a lot of it."

He then looked at Ann, put his wig back on, and smiled. "Sorry, Granddaughter, you have to recognize that women don't have the monopoly on vanity; we men have some, too."

Ann was in shock. Anger gave way to surprise. Surprise gave away to a surge of affection and she ran up, embraced her grandfather. "I never knew why you were so touchy about your hair. You are such a marvelous grandfather."

She embraced him then turned to Joe. "You're wonderful, too, Joe."

Chapter XV
Hoodwinked?

Joe both liked and disliked his new job as Deputy Squadron Commander. The promotion meant more money. As a major with flight pay, he was able to save quite a bit, half of which he put into bonds and half of which he sent home to invest in the farm. He didn't like the increase in paperwork, but Armentrout was a first-rate C.O. who demanded that either Joe or he be at the base during every mission. Joe flew half the missions and Armentrout the other half. As the weeks went by, Joe's tally moved from five German planes to six then seven plus a number of cripples, which he let the junior pilots make the kill on. The other pilots thought his letting the newer pilots finish off the cripples was unselfish, but in reality, Joe knew he didn't want to do it. One night when Joe came back from a mission, he went into the office.

Armentrout smiled. "Have time to sit and chat?"

"Sure." Joe slouched into a chair.

Armentrout dragged on his cigarette then blew a smoke ring. "Kind of lonesome now that Ann has gone back to Cambridge, aren't you?"

"Yeah."

"What are you doing with your spare time?"

"Reading."

"What are you reading?"

"I've been reading Caesar and his tactics in the Gallic Wars. You have any West Point textbooks left around? I sure would like to read them."

"I have a few with me. You're welcome to them. What did you learn from Caesar and Napoleon?"

"Same thing you learn from every great general – surprise. Come at them where they can't see you and hit them first with the most. That's essentially what that whole Kraut blitzkrieg was all about."

"You're right. It's true in air combat, too. Seems to me we need to be a little bit more original."

"I think we can be a little more original, a little more aggressive. From what I've heard of the new P-47s and the P-51s that are coming, we're going to have stuff that is equal to or better than anything the Krauts have."

"We're going to need to think about how to use them, too. I'm sending you down to Duxford for an orientation on both the new P-47s and the new P-51s. I want you to learn all you can about them. I'm leaving you there a week."

"Great."

Armentrout smiled at him. "Don't think I don't know what that grin is about. Duxford is close to Cambridge."

When Joe arrived at Duxford, he found that both the new P-51 and the new P-47 with their bubble canopies, longer range, and drop tanks were much superior to anything they'd been flying. He was flat-out excited. It would be awhile until they had enough of either one, but when they did, they would have the advantage.

On the first night that he was free, he decided to exercise his surprise plan on Ann. He had thought it out in detail and talked with her over the phone about trying mental telepathy. If they were really in love, she should be able to feel what he feels even though they were separated by distance.

He went into Cambridge and called her from a phone across the street from her dorm where he could see her. He told her to go out on the east porch at 7 o'clock and face the direction of their airbase, close her eyes, meditate, and see if she could feel and hear his thoughts and respond. Ann reluctantly agreed.

He watched until she went out on the porch and faced the other way. She had instructions to close her eyes, bow her head, and concentrate intently on Joe. She faced toward the base, directly away from where Joe was watching and bowed her head. He could see that she was in deep concentration. He quietly crossed the street, silently crept around in front of her, and whispered, "Can you hear my voice? Can you feel me near you in thought? Are we communicating?"

She answered softly, "Yes," then raised her head and he saw a piece of paper taped to her face with a hole for each eye, a hole for her nose, and a hole for her mouth. Written across the paper in wide lipstick letters was: *How stupid do you think I am?*

Joe burst out laughing. "I thought I had you hoodwinked."

"How could you have me hoodwinked when every call from the base is full of static and a call from close by comes in clear? Anyway, to be completely honest, I had a letter from Maggie McQuire saying that you were going to be detached down here. I was sorry I hadn't heard from you earlier."

"They didn't give me any time, and I wanted to surprise you."

"Joe, why are you so silly? What was it that made you want to pull a prank like that on me?"

"It was worth it. I had all the fun of conjuring up how I was going to hoodwink you, and then you had the fun of hoodwinking me. It looks to me like we both win."

"Maybe you're right. At least life with you is never going to be dull. I don't understand why Crole and Armentrout think you're dull. I think they're dull compared to you."

"Hang on to that bias, will you?"

Chapter XVI
Checking Up

Ann's mother and father, George and Sarah Bradford, were living in a flat in downtown London during the war. Their house in the suburbs was one of many now in use by the military. Her father was a successful financier in London. He had taken a Deputy Minister position in the government to help in the war effort. Her mother was giving full-time to the Red Cross. The brothers were in the service. All of them wanted to keep Ann in school rather than volunteering for one of the female organizations. They particularly appreciated having her at Bradford Hall to help the Brigadier in the summer. But now they had serious issues to talk about.

"Sarah, I've been doing some checking on this young man, Joe Oberlin."

"What have you found out? I really want to know. If he lives, I think it's very likely Ann will marry him."

"From what you've heard of him from Ann, what do you think of him, Sarah?"

"I think he must be an unusually strong individual and quite different. Frankly, I think Ann is totally smitten. I didn't ever think she would fall this hard this fast."

"It hasn't been all that fast. It's been a good many months."

"I hope you have good news because if you don't we're going to be in trouble."

"I think we have good news. I do hate the thought of his not being British, and I don't like it a bit that he's in such a high-risk military unit, but I'll tell you what I know, and then you tell me what you know.

"I got in touch with his commanding officer, who happened to be in London last week, and had a chance to chat with him. He's a strange chap, a West Pointer, a real military power type. I'm sure he'll be a general some day. He's a little unusual as he talks about Joe. Joe is his deputy, yet he seems to be awed by Joe.

"He tells me he wasn't fair to Joe starting out, that he held him back from a promotion. He believed anybody that didn't smoke, drink, or behave badly with women was a coward. He told other people Joe was yellow, and all the time he didn't know that Joe had shot down four Japanese airplanes and had several medals.

"He said Joe saved his life; he would be dead if it weren't for Joe. He says that doesn't seem to matter to Joe. He never pays any attention to it. It was something, you know. He shot down three airplanes when he was so badly wounded no one could believe he could fly. He just can't figure Joe out.

"Then this chap, Armentrout, told me to get in touch with a man named Crole. Said Crole was Joe's best friend; he could tell me more about him than anyone else.

"I rang up this man Crole, told him that the Colonel had told me to call him. Crole is a strange one; he likes to exaggerate. He just boomed right out, said Joe is the best man in the Army Air Corps bar none. He says he's a good pilot, good man, religious square, thinks about heavy stuff, is tediously dull part of the time, but a good man to have around to put you to bed when you're drunk. They call him the Cube because any way you look at him he's a square. He said he's the best if you can put up with worrying about the future of the human race and can understand a man who will spend an evening reading history or the Bible instead of getting drunk at the Officer's Club.

"That Crole is a charming chap. He says, 'If you're worried about your daughter, forget it. The guy is a complete square, thinks the world of your daughter. Joe wouldn't begin to think about marriage until the war was over because he couldn't stand the thought of a lovely creature like her being a widow, and his business is too high risk. You can breathe easy if that's what's on your mind. She's safer with him than she would be if she was locked up in a safe.' Now what do you think, Mary?"

"I think we couldn't be luckier. I just hope he appreciates her brain. She's our outstanding scholar and should be encouraged to do great things. Seems to me we are as safe as we could hope to be, and time will tell us what to do. If that man survives the war —

and that is a big if — Ann will marry him. And if she does, our daughter will be overseas in the middle of the United States."

"Well, you can look at it this way, Sarah, we always wanted to see the States; we'd have a home base to travel from."

Chapter XVII
Surprise

Joe was surprised when he got the message to report to Col. Armentrout on the double.

Joe saluted. Armentrout looked serious. "Joe, pack your bag; be sure to take your best uniform. You're due out of here in twenty minutes."

"What are you talking about?"

"Orders, just now got them. You're due out of here in twenty minutes. You're going to the States."

"For how long?"

"Don't know. Probably not very long. You're just ordered out of here. That's all I can tell you. Get your gear, there's going to be a B-17 stopping in shortly to pick you up. You're on your way, man. Have a good time."

"Thank you, sir. Is this good news or bad news?"

"You'll find out when you get there. Last time they called you there, they sent you from the Pacific theater to Europe. I doubt if they'll send you the other way this time. Maybe they just want to pick your brains. But get with it, man, you're almost out of time."

Joe saluted, almost forgetting to drop the other fingers. The Colonel saluted and dropped the other fingers. Joe turned and started off at a trot. The Colonel chuckled as the door banged.

It was a long haul in the back of a B-17 with stops at Iceland and Gander, Newfoundland, Maine, and then D.C. They didn't need to make quite that many stops for fuel, but it was a milk run where they picked up things and left things off. When they landed at Andrews Air Base, there was a staff car waiting.

A spit and polish major walked up to Joe. "Major Oberlin, come with me."

They put him up in the officer's quarters. The major assigned to him looked him over very closely and snapped, "We'll get you a haircut. We had better get you a little fresher uniform than that. We'll have it ready by morning."

They had him measured that evening. The next morning, hanging in his room was a new uniform with all his ribbons and up-to-date service bars on it.

When he came downstairs, he met a colonel who informed him that he was to accompany him and that they were due at the White House in an hour. Joe took another quick look in the mirror and at his hands, glad his fingernails were clean and that he had a reasonable haircut, the best they could do with the scars. They took off in a staff car driving to the White House, going through the usual security with the colonel taking care of all that.

They were ushered into a waiting room. Ten minutes later, the door opened and in walked his mother, his father, his sister Annie, and Uncle Ed. He jumped up with excitement, embracing each one, and saying, "What on earth is this all about?"

"We aren't supposed to tell, but we're excited."

The door opened and the colonel spoke softly, "Follow me, please. Bring the four of them with you, Major."

They were escorted into the East Room where Joe was led to a line consisting of a Marine Corps staff sergeant in a wheelchair with both legs gone, a sailor who showed scars over the side of his head and one sleeve hung empty, a couple of other men showing no obvious injuries, and two young ladies who were alone.

Joe leaned over to the colonel. "What's this all about?"

The colonel softly answered, "The President will be here shortly. Come sharp to attention, salute when your name is called."

Joe, mystified by what was going on, was still mystified when the President wheeled in. He read a citation for each man. As they went down the row, each man was presented with the Congressional Medal of Honor, the ribbon was hung around their neck, and they were congratulated by the President. Two were posthumous. The widows were standing there, tear streaked, as they were handed the medals.

When they came to Joe, the President read the citation, congratulated him, and hung the medal around his neck. The President asked, "Is there anything you would like to say?"

"Thank you, sir. I don't deserve this. Many men have done much more than I have. The real heroes of this war are dead. I accept it as an undeserving recipient. Thank you."

The President smiled warmly, as he was wheeled from the room. The White House staff invited the group to a reception in the next room.

As they went to the other room, Joe could hardly wait to hear the news from his family not having seen them for two years. There was intense chatter. As they were sitting in a group, Annie, the ever-loving little sister who had made Joe feel like such a hero when he was such a bust, stood up, walked around where Joe was sitting, and began to closely examine the scars on his head and on his cheek. She looked him in the eye as she spoke. "Joe." Then she put her pointer finger on his nose. "Don't you let those bad guys shoot you anymore."

Joe laughed and the whole family laughed, but what they didn't know was that an AP photographer had picked it up and had taken a perfect shot of the gesture. A newsreel camera picked up the whole thing on film and their microphone had picked up what she said. Joe need not worry about publicity because the story and the picture were a sensation. The media always had an eye for a beautiful girl and Annie was beautiful. It caught the whimsy of a nation of Al Capp readers. Annie and Joe's nose became famous while the medal went almost unnoticed.

The family was staying at the Mayflower. Joe had to fly back early the next morning. They arranged a private dining room where they could have a table just for their family and chatted long into the evening.

Mother repeatedly saying, "Don't you need to get some rest, Joe?"

Joe always replied, "I can sleep on the plane and I can't talk with you people on the plane."

Annie asked, "Joe, do you still have that weird dream about the huge flash, a plane spiraling down, and then nothing?"

"Yes, more frequently recently."

Chris smiled. "Joe, you have such funny dreams."

Ed Riley felt the skin tighten on his face, but he said nothing.

The highlight of the evening from Joe's point of view was when a chance came to say what was in his heart. "I want to thank all of you so much. This is not my medal today. This is our medal, our medal as a family, our medal as a unit, and our medal as an army. But what I want to thank you for is 'we'. During those horrible years when we thought we were going to lose the farm, it was always 'us'. When I had so much trouble in school, Annie made me her hero. Uncle Ed teaching me to fly is why I ended up where I am.

"You loved no matter what, and it carried me through a lot of rough times. Dad, I think about you and Mom a lot. When I was young, you took me into your confidence and told me the hard truth. You were tough. If we don't look at reality like reality is, we can't succeed. Matter-of-fact, in the business I'm in, you can't live.

"Looking at reality helped me when a lot of other guys couldn't do it.

"Then you had the strength and generosity to let go. You let me go into business with Uncle Ed and then hired other kids to take my place. But perhaps," and his gaze changed as he looked at the whole family, "perhaps more than anything else it was never any one or another; it was always us. We all believed. We believed in our country and ourselves. The things we believed were more important than we were.

"The guys back on the base would laugh at this, but I want to propose a toast with water. It's a double toast. The first one is to Aunt Eve who taught us how to see the good in people." All eyes moistened and a tear dropped from Uncle Ed's chin as they drank the toast. And then he added, "And the second one is to us."

Chapter XVIII
Change

Things were getting fluid with the Army Air Corps in Britain. Pilots were coming in, mostly fresh out of transition — all new to combat. Officers were being reassigned right and left; Armentrout was jerked out and made a brigadier general. Crole promoted out of his squadron and made Chipman's number two and Joe found himself now a bird colonel commanding the squadron. He honed his men hard on his basic philosophies pointing out again and again that it was true from Caesar to Napoleon to now: Be organized, be disciplined, be tough. Surprise them if you can, hit 'em hard and fast, get there first with the most.

The joy was that Ann was back at Bradford Hall, but the sad thing was that as a commanding officer he had less time off and was a little uncomfortable when he took any. This was partially offset by the fact that as a C.O. he had some latitude. The Brigadier had taken an increasing interest in the Army Air Corps; so, he was often able to have Ann and the Brigadier join him for dinner. He always had them present for any kind of ceremonies; they beefed up the audience and the troops liked the idea of having a good-looking lady as well as a British war hero showing their respects when various medals were handed out or other special events were commemorated.

Ann was particularly excited to be present for Maggie McQuire's promotion to major. Maggie needed it. Ever since Armentrout left, she had been very lonely and found many excuses to get to Bradford Hall to visit Ann. Ann and Maggie were as different as Joe and Armentrout, but like the two men, their differences seemed to foster the friendship. It excited Ann to hear Maggie's almost motherly, protective attitude toward Joe and her violent defense of Joe at the faintest innuendo of criticism.

One rainy evening, Joe walked into the Officer's Club and found the usually buoyant Crole sitting alone almost in tears.

"What's the matter, Crole?"

"Shit!"

"Now that you have enlightened me with your learned vocabulary, tell me what's the matter."

Crole banged the table with his fist. "Damn, dirty, stinking war kills the good guys."

"What happened?"

"Dzewaltowski bought it."

"What happened?"

"His B-17 was shot up. He brought it in anyway. The landing gear collapsed and it blew up!"

"I always liked Charlie."

"I know. When they used to call his name from a written list he got tired of pronouncing it right – Jiveltofski – then you would pronounce it for him and they would confuse him with you."

Joe's eyes grew moist. "I thought he appreciated my doing that."

"I know he did. He took it as showing friendship."

"They say the good die young. I'm starting to believe it."

"I've been sitting here counting up. Of those I can account for in our class at Kelly Field, over half are dead and several are all busted up."

"Did you ever wonder if we have burned up more than our share of good luck?"

Crole's eyes lit up. "I think about that a lot in lots of ways."

"Like what?"

"Like every time an infantry officer twenty years older than I am salutes me because I outrank him."

"We can't help that. The Air Corps grew fast and killed off too many pilots. All we had to do was be where we were early in the war and stay alive."

"If I were in the ground forces, I would hate saluting some smart-ass punk who was half my age."

Joe swirled his iced tea and stared at it. "I know what you mean. Sometimes, it seems to me that we are reaping the benefits of so many friends getting killed."

"Seems like! Hell, man, we are."

Joe was morose. "When you look at the whole picture, it stinks. Look at our kill ratios, and think of how many men die just because they were born in the wrong place."

"Cube, stop that bullshit. This is war and it's kill or be killed. If you dwell on that kind of stuff, it will drive you nuts."

"Here comes Ann. Join us for dinner and we can both bleed on her. With a few more beers and some time with us, you'll feel better."

As the evening wore on and Crole drank more, he became more talkative.

"Cube, you are stupid. You are sitting there with a beautiful woman, stone sober, and still hurting over Charlie. I'm half drunk and happy. You'll work your butt off and never be rich, but at least once a week, I hang one on and I'm as rich as John D. Rockefeller."

"I don't have to fight hangovers, I save some money, and I'm not as likely to run over someone getting home."

"Hell, man, you're stupid. Chances are we'll both be killed. I'll die having experienced life and riches, and you'll die a poor virgin."

Ann smiled and Joe laughed.

"Ann, you have just heard from the Air Corps' Socrates. Don't bother with bringing up such things as deferred gratification or the peace that comes from Christian commitment. It won't wash with him."

A whimsical smile came over Crole's face. "Damn squares, I don't know why I love you so much. You're really dull as hell!"

The next morning, Sarah Bradford's phone rang. "Mum?"

"Ann, dear."

"I need to talk."

"Thanks for calling. It's flattering."

"I had a bad night."

"Why?"

"I had dinner with Joe and Crole."

"That should have been delightful."

"It was, but it really wasn't."

"Why?"

"I learned that over half of their class has been killed."

"That's worse than I thought."

"Those two are so different, yet there is a bond that is a sort of super brotherhood. It's more than they would fight and die for each other, that each has things the other doesn't have, or that opposites attract. I can't explain it. It is covered with demeaning remarks and ridicule, but you get the impression if you stood on one man's foot the other man's arm would fly up."

"I have gathered some of that kind of thing from your grandfather when he talks about soldiers in the last war. Does this worry you?"

"No. That's not what I called about."

"Go on."

"I have a hard time thinking that Joe might be killed."

"You have known that all along."

"But I didn't know how high the risk was."

"Is that what ruined your night?"

"No, that's only a part of it."

"Go on."

"Crole was drunk. He said since he sleeps with women and feels rich when he gets drunk, if he is killed, he will die having experienced life and riches; if it happens to Joe, he'll die a poor virgin."

"What did Joe say?"

"Not much. But after Crole left, he told me he thought Crole was much like his Uncle Ed was before he met his Aunt Eve. Then he said his Uncle Ed had told him he had never really been alive until he met Aunt Eve and her faith."

"Did he say anything else?"

"He said if Crole had seen and felt what he had seen and felt with his parents and family, Crole would feel differently."

"Did he say more?"

"Only that we should appreciate Crole. He is actually happy that Crole has shot down more planes than he has. I think that's because Crole feels good about it and Joe is very uncomfortable about war and killing."

"What's bothering you, Ann?"

"That bit about Joe dying without having fully lived life. Do you think I should push Joe to get married? He hasn't asked me, but I know he will. We have talked."

"What does Joe say?"

"He says longer courtships make better marriages. He says we really wouldn't have enough time together to make it a real marriage till after the war and that this is a chance to have a mental oneness to get the bumps out of the road for a real marriage."

"Did Crole ever say anything?"

"I think Crole worries some about that dream Joe keeps having about the flash, the spiral, and then oblivion. Lots of pilots are superstitious. Once, when he was drunk, he said that Joe loved me too much to marry me and leave second-hand goods if he was killed."

"What do you think?"

"I think Joe is right, but it's scary to be such odd balls in a war when everyone seems to grab the pleasure of the moment."

"Are you still afraid of the animal part of you?"

"No. I understand it for what it is, but I watch it. Joe said it's like fire. In the stove where it belongs, it keeps you warm and does other good things, but if you let it out, it burns the house down and ruins everything."

Sarah Bradford laughed. "Joe is one of a kind. What do you really want to do, Ann?"

"I want to wait till after the war, but I don't want to cheat Joe."

"You won't be. That's clearly what he wants, too."

"What if he's killed?"

"He dies knowing he did what he thought best."

"Thanks, Mum. Any thoughts?"

"Only that the fire in the stove is a marvelous thing."

"I love you, Mum. Bye, bye."

"Bye, bye. You are a lovely daughter."

Sarah Bradford hung up and muttered, "How lucky can one mother be?"

Chapter XIX
Combat Fatigue

Times were hard for Joe. The new P-51s with their auxiliary tanks were a problem. They gave long-range escort to the heavy bombers. That's a great thing for the bombers, but it didn't take the Germans long to figure out that those auxiliary tanks gave them a competitive advantage as long as the fighter hung on to them.

Joe popped in to see the flight surgeon. "Mac, do you have time to talk?"

"Sure, Colonel, what is it?"

"I need some advice. I've watched a lot of squadron commanders burn out. I don't want to burn out. When I feel the load I'm carrying, I know I could. The missions help a lot. I think they're good for me, but so many administrative things come up I don't get to go as much as I want.

"There is something that keeps eating on me — it's the killing. I know we have to win the war and we have to protect each other, but I believe killing is wrong. When someone shoots down an enemy, there is celebration. I go along with it, but in my gut I can't help feeling for the parents or widow of that pilot. Some bail out, but a lot don't.

"I try to play volleyball with the guys and that helps. I run some and I read, but when I'm reading I sometimes have trouble concentrating on the reading because thoughts of the day creep in. As you know, I believe in prayer, and I even find those thoughts slipping into my prayer time. I don't think that's good, Doc. I think if I don't figure out how to handle this it's going to wear me down."

The doctor looked at him. "I think you're right, Joe. That's why a lot of men go to booze. That only helps short term; it doesn't last and doesn't cure. I think savoring hanging one on probably does more for them than actually hanging one on. What do you have that really gives you a thrill?"

"It's always a thrill to see Ann, but she's gone back to Cambridge. I do get a thrill when I call her up from time to time, but she has to study and she's a long way off."

"Are you engaged to the girl?"

"No, but I hope to be."

"She's a lovely girl."

"Yeah, but this isn't answering my question, Doc. How do I tell when it's gettin' to me? How do I tell when I'm near the edge?"

"The fact that you're worried about the edge is a good sign, Joe. If you know you could fall, you're in a lot better shape than those who think they can't and then fall off. I don't think you will, but you need to think about it because it's going to cut your efficiency when you get preoccupied and it will cut down your creative thinking. One thing that makes you a good C.O. is that you think new. I know you worry about the losses, any C.O. does, but your kill/loss ratio is excellent."

"Yeah, but we're missin' the subject. How do you deal with it?"

"The first thing I think you need to do is realize you're too tough on yourself. You insist your men take time off, but you don't take any for yourself. I suggest you just tell the Wing C.O. that on doctor's orders you're going to go down and see Ann for a long weekend every so often. That will help. I'd also suggest you come in and blow off steam to me. I'm no shrink, but it's good to talk and you can always talk in medical confidence to me. I'd do the same thing with the chaplain. There you're not talking line duty and you can talk about what eats your guts. Everybody has to talk about what eats his guts. Since Crole went to the other squadron, you don't have that kind of a buddy talk very often. Use us, that's what we're here for."

"I'll do it. Thanks a lot. I feel better already."

Chapter XX
Betrayed?

Joe reflected on his conversation with the flight surgeon, as he walked to the Officer's Club. He went through the door and saw Crole at the far end, obviously with enough beer in him to be feeling good, having a really chummy chat with one of the nurses who had had a little more beer than he had.

"Hi, Crole. Hi, Mary."

"Hi, Cube. How are you?"

"A little under the weather, I guess. I miss Ann."

"Betcha do."

"Crole, when can you and I have a chat? I need to talk to you."

"Any time. How about now?"

"Don't want to take you away from Mary." He glanced at Mary and saw her lower lip pucker.

"That's okay. Mary has a lot of friends here. Why don't we go for a walk?"

As the door banged behind them, Crole looked at Joe. "You look like something the cat dragged in. What's the matter?"

"Had a chat with the flight surgeon, been losing some sleep. Got to thinking about all the other senior pilots and how so many of them are showing combat fatigue. A lot of them even caving in. A few of them, like the Aussies say, went 'round the bend. I haven't slept very well the last few nights. I keep thinking about killing. It's still wrong — it's just less wrong than seeing your buddies killed. Began to wonder if it was taking a toll on me. How you feeling, Crole?"

"Oh, sorta the same way. Although, when I can hang one on and go down and flirt with people like Mary, it helps a lot. You miss a lot with no cigarettes and no booze. It does a lot for those of us who know how to live."

"To each his own. You may have the easier system, but mine has always worked for me. Do you see any signs of wear and tear in me?"

"Yeah, some. You don't laugh as much as you did, but I figured that was 'cause Ann went back to school, or 'cause of that dream you keep having, or maybe it's the weight of command."

"You have weight, too. Like me, you command the whole shooting match every other day. It's an awful thing to realize that we're responsible for all those other guys. They're all like brothers."

"Weighs on me, too."

"Crole, the flight surgeon says I ought to take time off and go down and see Ann. Do you think I should do it?"

"Hell, yes."

"I'm not so sure."

"What has gotten into you, Cube? Here's doctor's orders to do what you want to do more than anything else in the world and you're not sure. What's the matter?"

"I didn't hear from Ann last week, called her three times this week, and she hasn't returned my calls. Wonder if she's hacked off at me. I can't figure out what's wrong. I hope I haven't stubbed my toe."

"Doubt if you have. She's a pretty true-blue type. Don't think she'd ever get interested in anybody else, but if she did, she'd sure be up front about it."

"I just don't know. Funny how life works; almost always when you're in a lot of stress one place you get a lot of stress in another."

"Stop that crap. Go down and see her. She'll pick you up."

"Thanks, Crole. I miss having more time with you. You always sort of pulled me out."

"You're a stiff bastard, but you always pulled me out, too."

"Thanks for your guidance. Better let you get back to Mary. Seemed like you were making a lot of headway there."

Crole gave his impish grin, did an about face, and trotted off toward the club. Joe went back and arranged to get a plane the next day, so he could fly to Duxford to see Ann.

Joe called Ann; again, she wasn't in. He left word again for her to call him and added, "I really need to talk to you."

He then went to his room hoping to get a phone call; none came and he went to sleep.

The next afternoon he landed at Duxford, picked up a jeep, drove into Cambridge, and stopped at Ann's dorm.

The dorm mother looked at him in a friendly, guarded way. "I'm sorry, Ann isn't in. She won't be in until probably about ten o'clock which is closing hours."

"Do you know where I could find her?"

"No, I don't. She didn't say. She's been very busy lately."

Joe left and drove down to a local pub known for its good food. He sat in one of the deep-walled booths and ordered dinner. The pub had booths designed for intimate conversations and Joe could hear very little of the noises of the other patrons. Before his dinner arrived, he rose to go to the men's room. He looked on the opposite side and saw Ann sitting there with a very handsome, bearded, young naval officer. They were obviously intently engaged in an intimate conversation, so he said nothing and went on to the men's room.

When he emerged, he felt he had been a little foolish in walking on by, so he walked up to their booth excited at seeing Ann and smiling broadly. Ann was so engrossed in her conversation she didn't see him. The young naval officer looked up a couple of times while still listening intently to Ann.

Joe stood there a minute and heard Ann say, "I love you. I have loved you for as long as I can remember and I love you intently. The happy memories of our times together are burned permanently into my heart and nothing can erase them. I hope that you feel the same way. Think of the wonderful times, like the times when we slept in the woods."

Joe's face went from smile to blankness to anger, and he wheeled and walked away not bothering to think about his ordered dinner. He jumped in his jeep, drove out to Duxford, got in his plane, flew directly back to the base, and told his deputy, "I'll lead the squadron tomorrow."

He then went to the Officer's Club, saw Crole again feeling a few beers and enjoying himself. "Crole, I need to talk to you."

They went out the door. "I'm gunshot."

Crole was confused. "Whatta ya talkin' about?"

Joe told him. Crole was skeptical. "Somethin' doesn't register. She's not that kind. You're making too much judgment, too fast."

"What would you do?"

"Oh, I'd be mad as hell. I'd be screamin' mad, but I'm not you, Joe. Since I'm not you, I can be more objective. If it were me having that kind of trouble, you'd be the same way. We both know Ann and we both know she isn't that kind, so there's somethin' doesn't fit."

"I arranged to command the flight tomorrow."

"Why?"

"Because it's the one place I can forget about all this stuff. Don't worry. I won't let it interfere. I'll keep my cool."

"Are you sure of that?"

"Yeah."

"I think you're right. I think that's the thing to do. You will keep your cool, the guys need you, and when you get enough adrenaline running in you it'll wipe out any of that fatigue. Maybe when the dust settles we'll know what's goin' on. Doesn't she have a brother in the navy?"

"Yes, but she told me three or four times he's in the Mediterranean and he won't be back for two months."

"I thought so. You never know. They might have taken a torpedo or gotten hit with a bomb and come back early, so don't jump to so many conclusions. Don't blow it and lose a girl like that."

Crole looked at him with compassion and whimsy. "You're bitin' off too much too soon. Those Bradfords are a clannish bunch, and if her brother had some kind of a crisis, she'd count on you being strong enough to handle things on your own and unhook to bail him out. Don't make judgment. Keep your options open. Think about something else."

"Thanks, Crole. You always had more sense than I did under all your nonsense."

Crole grinned and headed back for the club.

#

Ernest Bradford listened with appreciation to what Ann had to say and then spoke gently. "Ann, I think you're missing something."

Ann withdrew from her intentness. "What are you talking about?"

"A good-looking Army Air Corps officer came up smiling and looking at you with what seemed to be great affection. He stood there for quite a little while, as you told me how much you loved me. His face changed from smile, to blankness, to anger, and he walked off."

Ann's face blanched. "What did he look like?"

"Good-looking chap, tall, had a scar on the side of his head. The scar looked recent. Walked like he was a man in the habit of command."

"What did he have on his shoulders?"

"I think he was a colonel."

"Oh, heavens!"

"What's the matter, Ann?"

"He knows that my brother is in the Mediterranean. I told him so. Told him you wouldn't be back for two months. I didn't tell him you were here because you told me not to tell anybody we were talking. Think what he'll think, particularly with that comment about sleeping in the woods."

She dropped everything and ran to the door in time to hear a jeep zooming towards the airbase. She came back in panic. "Oh Ernie, I haven't returned his phone calls. I've been too busy talking with you. Your problem is so awful. I look at Joe as indestructible. I look at Joe as somebody who can take anything. I've neglected him. I've ignored him. I haven't been fair to him. What should I do?"

Ernie was thoughtful. "I came up here to get your advice and it's been good. I was just ready to tell you I've decided what I'm going to do. I'm going to get a divorce."

"Are you sure that's what you want to do?"

"I'm absolutely sure."

She looked at him. "Ernie, when you asked that other officer to spend the night in your flat, are you sure you weren't really expecting to find her with another man and expecting a bad situation where you'd need a witness?"

Ernie smiled faintly. "No, I'm not sure. As a matter of fact, in our conversations, I've wondered about that a lot. I needed to talk to you because you're the only one who talked sense to me before I married her. The rest of the family just didn't like her, but you liked her. You did warn me that you thought she was too weak to be a naval officer's wife and she couldn't handle stress. Since you were right the first time, I thought you'd be right this time. You haven't told me what to do, but in talking with you, I know what to do because I could never go to sea again in peace. I don't think she's really capable of the kind of love we have in our family. The only thing to do is get a divorce."

Ann, for the first time, expressed an opinion. "You know, Ernie, it hurts me to say this for her sake, but I think you're absolutely right. Now, you tell me, what am I going to do about the mess I'm in?"

"I doubt if it's as bad as you think because he knows you have a brother in the navy. When he finds out I came back early, and particularly since I've made up my mind and you can tell him what we were talking about, he'll understand that. He will admire you for it. The question is what happens between now and when you get a chance to talk to him. I suggest you go back, call him, and hope the phone circuits aren't jammed."

"I'll do that. He'll be airborne by now, so there's no point in not finishing dinner, but I haven't written him, I haven't returned his phone calls, and I've been cruel. I mustn't take people for granted even when they're strong and tough as Joe is."

When Ann went back, the circuits were jammed and she couldn't get through, but worse than that, she read Joe's message: *I need to talk to you.*

That night, when Joe didn't get a phone call, he reflected it was probably a brother thing, but the truth of the matter was he said he needed her and she didn't respond. He needed to think about that some more but not tonight. He better get a good night's sleep. He had a big day tomorrow and he dropped off to sleep.

The next morning, as he felt the exhilaration of his engine roaring, the camaraderie of taking off, and forming up in formation, all thoughts of his problems were gone. There was brotherhood in these friends risking their lives. The orders of the day were to escort bombers on a short run. On the way back, half of them were authorized to peel off and seek out targets of opportunity. The flight turned out to be a milk run.

On the way back, Joe called Haman the B-Flight commander. "You baby-sit the mother hens; I'm going down with A Flight and see if we can do something to the bad guys."

They peeled off to low altitude. Joe called on the mike. "Loosen up the formation, keep your eyes open. Let's get something worthwhile."

About halfway to the coast, Joe came on again. "Look at that train ahead. Let's get it. I'll go in first. You guys cover me. I'll peel out and cover you until we've shot it up." Then with a chuckle, thinking of his British friends, he yipped, "Tally ho," and dove on the train.

He pressed the firing button. He watched his tracers spurt toward the train and saw spouts of steam come out of the engine. His bullets ripped into the other cars. As he proceeded down toward the middle of the train, there was a tremendous explosion and he instantly pulled hard back on the stick.

Smoke and flying debris engulfed his P-51, as he felt a concussion that lifted the plane violently upward. How high he was he didn't know. He felt debris plow into his plane and marveled that the Merlin engine could still function, but as he continued to climb, it began to run rough. He saw his oil pressure dropping and his other instruments malfunctioning. The engine got rougher; and just as he was sure it was going to die, he pulled back the canopy, flipped upside down, dropped out, and promptly yanked his ripcord. The next thing he felt was a violent jerk, as the parachute opened; seconds later, he felt leaves, limbs, twigs, and then a violent thump and passed out.

Chapter XXI
Escape

The next day, Crole called Ann. "Ann, bad news. Joe's down. Doesn't look good. The other fellows flew around and watched closely, saw the plane where it smashed in the ground, no sign of any parachute anywhere and only a couple of French farmers pitching hay onto a wagon with a young woman driving the horse. Had there been a chute the Frenchies would have done something, but they weren't paying attention to anything. Our guys saw a truck full of Kraut soldiers headed toward the crash site, but it didn't appear they were going to find anything. I don't want you to give up hope, but honestly, it doesn't look good."

Ann sobbed. "Crole, did I kill him?"

"What are you talking about?"

"I was telling my brother how much I loved him. He is going through a horrible situation, and Joe came up to the table and I didn't even see him. I had told Joe that my brother was in the Mediterranean. I've been so involved in my brother's problems that I hadn't written Joe. I hadn't returned his phone calls. When I tried to call him last night I couldn't get through. Did he think I had ratted out on him or I was unfaithful, and therefore, he didn't care and wasn't careful?"

Crole swallowed hard. "You don't need to worry about that one. We talked. I told him it was your brother. I asked him if the guy you were sitting with could look like your brother with a beard. I know he had seen his picture, and he said, yes, he could, but your brother was in the Mediterranean. I told him ships often get hit and come back early."

"Oh, Crole, that's exactly what happened. He came back early and surprised his wife; she was in the process of being unfaithful. Poor Ernest was devastated and came up to talk to me to decide what to do. I neglected Joe. I just took him for granted. You should never take anybody for granted. He needed me and I wasn't there for him. I feel horrible."

"Well, don't feel horrible that way. Let's just hope he made it some way. Don't ever give up. Don't ever say die. We may find out what happened — might even find out quicker than you think. People tell me that the French underground is one whale of an operation."

"Thank you, Crole. It's such awful news, but you've helped some. You've helped a lot, as a matter of fact. It's bad enough to grieve but to grieve with guilt would be unbearable. I feel some guilt but not as much as I would have."

"Don't feel any. If there's one thing Joe can do once he gets in that airplane, it's forget about all his personal problems and not worry about anything except the enemy and the guys he's flying with. I don't want to hurt your ego, but I can guarantee you that from the time he started that engine until whatever happened, happened your problem never crossed his mind."

"Oh, thank you, Crole. Bye."

"Bye. Bless you, Ann."

"Bless you, Crole."

#

Joe gradually became aware of the sense of confinement. He felt hard wooden boards underneath him and closeness, as his breath seemed to bounce off boards directly above him. He must have moaned because he quickly heard a young female French voice saying, "Monsieur, you must be quiet or all of us will be killed. If you turn to your side, you'll get more air because there's a hole in the bottom of the wagon. Don't be alarmed if you hear thumps. The Germans will probably probe the load of hay with their bayonets and hit the boards above you, but you must be quiet or we will all die. It shouldn't be long. Father hid your parachute before the smoke cleared."

Joe turned his head and was able to get a breath of fresh air. His hot, throbbing head felt like someone was hammering on it, and he gradually drifted back into sleep.

A few days later, Joe, with only vague memories of being in a farmer's basement, being fed, jostled, hidden in the bottom of wagons and in some cramped area in a canal boat, found himself in a hidden room in a small French port. He was sharing it with eight other men from the crew of a downed B-17 bomber. The others were bearing no side arms, but Joe had his 45. When their French host came to him, he took his 45 off and handed it to the Frenchman saying, "Thank you. You could put this to good use."

The Frenchman responded, "Oh, no, monsieur. Thank you, but if it were found in my possession, my life would be in much greater danger. Those in the most danger are those on the fishing boat who are going to take you into the channel. If German patrol boats find it, they'll kill all of you, kill the French crew, and destroy the boat. I suggest you keep it. If they do find you, it might help put up a fight."

The Frenchmen then left them food saying, "We'll be back to get you later."

As the door of the room closed, the bombardier from the bomber crew came up to Joe. "My name's Guder. I come from a German family. I spoke no English until I went to school, and I speak German as fluently as I do English. If we get caught, I might be able to be helpful in a fight. By speaking German, I might be able to keep them confused for a while until we could get some advantage.

"Might I suggest, sir, since you're the ranking officer here, that we see if we can acquire some heavy steel rods and some piano wire or good strong small ropes so that a boarding party might be overcome silently either using garrotes or steel rods to the head. If we were able to silently overpower them, a couple of us could get into their clothes. With my speaking German we might cause enough confusion to put up a good fight, at least good enough for the French to get away."

"Guder, that's good thinking. I was shot down once before in the South Pacific, and we had a couple of scraps before getting back."

They were able to acquire four iron bars about a foot long, a genuine piano wire, as well as a couple of small ropes.

Guder looked at the others. "I hope we don't have to use them, but if we do encounter a boarding party, it's really the only chance we have. Our formal armament is one 45. Hopefully, the Frenchies will have a gun or two, but we can't count on that."

A few hours later, they were crowded into the hold of a small French fishing boat that reeked of fish. They were chatting about 'what if' plans when the French captain stuck his head in. They told him what they had in mind in the event they encountered a German patrol boat.

The Frenchman smiled. "That's good because we all die any way, but it's better to die in a fight."

A few hours later, the French captain stuck his head in the hold again. "It is not good. With the engine off, we're making good headway under sail without any noise to attract the Germans, but the mist is clearing and the moon is brighter than I would like. It's better to have the sail than the noise, but we make more of a silhouette. This is not going to be an easy run. It is good that you have plans to fight."

Joe's appreciation of Guder had gone up considerably. The man was bright, alert, and understood the importance of surprise and the necessity of speed in getting the clothes off the Germans and on to Guder and his friends. Guder had wisely suggested that Gallagher, one of the bomber crew who was as strong as a bull, should be on one side of the companionway with a garrote and an agile man on the other side with an iron bar so as to move as promptly as possible when the boarding party came into the hold.

After a half hour of silent sailing, they were beginning to breathe easier when they heard the chug of what sounded like a diesel.

Joe glanced upward and saw the French captain at the helm clearly alarmed. He didn't expect that kind of diesel noise to come from the British smuggler who would probably be in a vessel much like their own. The sound boded no good.

Within about five minutes, a bright searchlight bore down on the French vessel and a loudspeaker boomed out, "Achtung!" followed by the English, "Halt! Stand by for boarding."

The Frenchmen responded with a torrent of French and the German responded in what appeared to Joe to be broken French, but it was clear from the tone that boarding was imminent.

The diesel patrol boat with a machine gun fore and aft promptly grappled with them. Three Germans in black sock caps, black coats, pants, and boots jumped onto the deck of the fishing boat. One went directly to the captain at the helm and began to interrogate him while two others came to the hatch of the hold and opened the door. One stuck his head in and began to descend the steps with the second following closely behind. When both of them were clearly below the level of the deck, there was a shuffling in the darkness. The first German let out a barely audible hum as he went down. Then came a thud followed by silence.

In a couple of minutes, Guder, dressed in German attire, stuck his head up the companion way gesturing vigorously for the

German who was interrogating the captain to come to him. Guder spoke softly to minimize personal identity. The other German responded quickly, followed Guder into the hold and there was a thud followed by the flop of a body.

A few minutes later, what appeared to be the three Germans came on deck, their guns pointing at six American airmen who held their hands in the air as their guards herded them towards the German patrol boat. The three 'German guards' — two with pistols, one with a submachine gun trained on the prisoners — waited on the fishing boat until the prisoners were on the deck of the German patrol boat.

As Guder and his men followed up the ladder, the German captain sensed something was not quite right as he looked at Guder and started to draw his pistol. Guder shot him on the spot. His helmsman reached for a pistol and Guder shot him. The German machine gunner on the rear machine gun, wheeled around to fire at the Americans, but Joe already had his 45 out from under his shirt and was able to put him out of action before he pulled the trigger. The real fear was the front gunner. Joe couldn't get a clean shot at him. Guder and his two henchmen couldn't get a clear shot either. The other Americans were about to be shot when there was a blast from the French fishing boat as a double-barreled shotgun blew the gunner away from his position.

Guder immediately ran into the hold of the patrol boat shouting loudly in German. There was a gunshot down below and a few minutes later Guder emerged with a prisoner in front of him.

Joe asked, "Do you think they got off a radio message?"

"I doubt it. I distracted them."

"How did you do that?"

"I confused them."

"How?"

"I ran down shouting in my best German, 'Where's the head? Where's the head? I gotta go now! I gotta go now!' Sensing my urgency, they took the time to point out where it was. One got suspicious and reached for a pistol. I shot him and turned on the other guy who threw his hands in the air. That's him; he's the radio operator. Says he didn't get off a message, but I think we have something worthwhile. See this weighted bag he had in his hand? At the start of the gunfire, he grabbed it. I suspect it's worth something, or they wouldn't want to throw it overboard so badly."

"See if you can find some way to put that man in irons, and let's get out of here. Set the course for Britain. We still have a lot of problems on our hands."

Joe turned to the French captain and saluted him. "Thank you, sir."

The Frenchman used his best English, "Thank you, sir. Any time. It was a pleasure to be your taxi."

The French boat peeled off, as Joe turned to the bomber crew. "We have to figure out how to get this idling engine into gear and head for England."

The bomber crew, having worked together for months, promptly went to work on the engine. Joe asked the bomber's radioman to check out the radio to see if he could get the frequencies they'd been operating on when he was flying. Shortly, the radioman came on deck saying it was an excellent radio, and he was confident he could reach the base. Joe gave him the frequency and asked for a mike.

Joe gave the call letters several times with no response, and then a rather sleepy voice came on.

"Liebewitz, this is the Cube. You wake up Crole and get him down there on the double. Tell him the Cube wants him on the horn now. When you get him, call back. Don't call till you have him. Clear."

In a few minutes, Crole's voice came on. "Cube, where in God's name are you?"

"Listen, Crole, only answer yes or no. Get that?"

"Yes, sir."

"Crole, remember where Maggie Brown's brother works?"

"Yeah."

"Well, we just acquired one of those using the Dillinger system. The response is going to be very much like O'Hara's was in your last poker game, so I need to get some stuff across with you quick. Remember where we got thrown out of the pub because you pinched the waitress' backside?"

"Yeah."

"Well, we're the same distance and the same direction from that place that the blond you used to date in flight school was from San Antonio. Got that?"

"Yeah."

"Write it down. Now we're gonna need what we give the big birds when bad guys are after 'em at the crack of dawn. Got that?"

"Yeah."

"Okay. This is a hot one, Crole. We've got some stuff that Ed Short would give his left one for, so we need to get there. Ya got it?"

"Yeah."

"Crole, do you remember what Sacajawea did?"

"Yeah."

"We need one of those. In addition to that, do you remember what color Sally Perkins' car was?"

"Yeah."

"Well, remember what the Yankees took out of the American League regularly?"

"Yeah."

"We'll have one of those and it will be the color of Sally Perkins' car. Got all that?"

"Yeah."

"Goin' out now. Don't want 'em to get a fix on the radio."

Crole turned to Liebewitz and snapped, "Get headquarters on the phone immediately."

Crole picked up the phone. "Colonel Oberlin has captured a German motor patrol boat. He is fifteen miles southeast of Dover expecting pursuit. He needs air cover at dawn. He needs a guide to get him through the minefields into a British port. The motor patrol boat will be flying a white pennant, and this whole matter is urgent because he is carrying highly sensitive intelligence information. With your permission, I'd like our squadron to give that air support in the morning. Please let me know as soon as possible."

Chapter XXII
Reconciliation

As dawn broke in the east, Joe heard Guder let out a shrieking, "Yippee." An instant later, he heard the roar of aircraft engines, as two P-51s passed over their boat and rocked their wings. With a little more light, Joe saw five more P-51s scouting the horizon at about ten thousand feet. Within an hour, a British patrol boat arrived with a pilot to get them through the minefields, and by noon, they were tying up to a dock in the Portsmouth naval yard with a band playing on the pier.

As they were securing the vessel, the band abruptly stopped and all present dismissed with instructions to tell no one of this boat. The whole episode was to be top secret.

Immediately, they tied a small boat fore and aft and spread canvas over the entire collection.

Joe recognized a bird colonel from Air Corps Intelligence standing on the dock next to a British naval captain, obviously his counterpart in intelligence for the British. The colonel was pointing to the newly painted writing down the side of the boat — Property of the U.S. Army Air Corps.

The colonel came aboard exclaiming, "Congratulations, Colonel Oberlin. This is a real accomplishment, but the whole event must be kept top secret. If the Germans find out we have captured their boat, any intelligence we get from it will be compromised. These fellows at the naval yard got a little carried away with enthusiasm, but it's under control and under cover now. I suspect that weighted bag has maps of their mine fields. We can't let them even suspect we have them."

Joe frowned. "Sir, I'd be happy to claim the credit if I could, but the credit all goes to these men and particularly to Lieutenant Guder. His innovative thinking and mastery of German pulled it off. The credit goes to him. I only fired one shot. I'm going to write Guder up for a Silver Star. He earned it.

"If you intelligence people move him into your operation, you'll not only get a fine mind, but he speaks perfect German. You'd better make him a captain quickly because he'll sure make it if he stays with us."

After about two hours of debriefing and questions about the weighted bag, Joe was free to go. Promptly, the handsome, bearded British naval officer he had seen talking with Ann the night he left the pub in anger confronted him.

"Colonel Oberlin?"

"Yes, sir."

"I'm Ernie Bradford, Ann's brother. I saw you but didn't get a chance to chat with you in Cambridge a few days ago."

"I remember it well."

"Would you do me the honor of having lunch on my ship? I command a destroyer. We're about fitted out, and I've arranged to have a private dinner with you on my ship if you would come with me. We have a lot to talk about."

"Thank you, I'd like to, but I'm filthy."

"That's all right. Heroes are entitled to be filthy."

Joe felt a knot in his stomach as the sight of falling Germans ran thru his memory. "I'm no hero. Guder did the whole thing. I merely went along for the ride and shot a German who was trying to save his shipmates."

"You look good to me and we need to talk. There will be a plane in here at 1500 hours to fly you back to your squadron; so, we don't have a lot of time. We can talk better on my ship."

"Okay."

As they sat in a small dining room in Ernie Bradford's destroyer, he looked at Joe and smiled wryly. "When I saw you the other night, did you recognize me as Ann's brother?"

"No. I'd been told you were in the Mediterranean."

"I thought so. You went from being very happy to being mad as hops before you stormed out. Did you think she was two-timing you?"

"I did at the time. It seemed so out of character for Ann, but I racked my mind and decided you had to be her brother. That bit about sleeping in the woods is what brought me to my senses. She'd told me about how the family used to go out in sleeping bags and sleep in the woods to listen to the night sounds and how her two big brothers told stories about wolves and bears and snakes and how she would edge her sleeping bag over towards her parents so you wouldn't notice she was scared."

Ernie laughed. "We noticed."

"I figured you did. I'd a done the same thing with my little sister."

"Now, Joe, I need to tell you something. Ann didn't write, didn't return your calls because she was saving my sanity. When my ship took a torpedo, we came back two months early, unexpectedly. I went to my apartment with a shipmate and found my wife in bed with another man. I was, needless to say, devastated. I needed to see Ann because she was the only one in my family who saw things correctly when I was married. I had to decide if I was going to sue for divorce or try to work some kind of reconciliation. I think Ann must have thought I was suicidal, and I can understand why she would because I was badly shaken.

After long discussions with Ann and days of meditation, I decided to get a divorce. I'm sure it's the right decision. I could never go to sea again without worrying, and she's probably happier without me anyhow. Now I can concentrate on my new command. I'm so excited about it that I don't worry much. But poor Ann is just about to die."

"What's the matter?"

"After you left, she ran out to try to catch you. She came back sobbing, 'Oh Ernie, he thinks you're in the Mediterranean. He'll believe I'm stepping out on him. I haven't written him and I haven't answered his phone calls, so he has every right to believe that.' When she went home and saw the message that you needed to talk to her, she tried to call you but couldn't get through.

"Then when your plane went down, she figured she'd broken your heart and killed you. I don't know what she would have done if your friend Crole hadn't told her that was nonsense. He said that he didn't want to hurt her feelings about how much you cared about her, but there was no way that you would have been thinking about that when you were in combat."

Joe thought a minute before he responded. "Funny how life works. I've been feeling guilty about storming out. I should have had complete faith in Ann. She's a straight arrow and never would step out on me. I really knew that in my gut. I was just worn out. Couldn't figure out what was going on. I'll have to admit when she was telling a good-looking naval officer that I had never seen before how much she loved him I couldn't quite handle it."

Ernie Bradford looked at Joe and smiled ruefully. "Believe me, I know how you felt."

Joe was embarrassed. "I have egg on my face. My telling you that is like a story my dad used to tell about a guy who had been in the Johnstown Flood. He died and went to heaven and was telling some old man how bad it was. The old man wouldn't pay any attention and walked off. He asked somebody else who the old man was and he said, 'That's Noah'."

Ernie laughed. "I've been told that you have a kind of Yankee, down-on-the-farm humor. I like it."

#

When Joe arrived at the airdrome, the pilot who was to fly him back to his squadron was confused. "I don't get these orders."

"What are you talkin' about?"

"I'm not ordered to fly you straight to the squadron. I'm supposed to fly to Duxford and wait there for a six-hour layover, and then fly you on to the base."

Joe inquired, "Whose orders?"

"Wing Commander. I know that Colonel Crole was calling him about something and the flight surgeon called him about something, but I don't know what's going on."

Joe grinned. "Enjoy the six hours at Duxford, I'm going to."

When the DC-3 landed at Duxford, Joe couldn't wait to find a jeep to get into Cambridge. He dropped the back door while the props were still blowing. As he held on to his hat and walked through the prop wash, the door of a U.S. Army staff car opened and he saw a blur rushing in his direction into the wind from the propellers. As she approached, he saw Ann's always immaculate hair blowing in every direction and found himself in a passionate embrace with a sobbing girl. Tears ran down his cheeks. Both kept saying I'm sorry, I'm sorry, I'm sorry.

As the engines stopped and the prop wash quit blowing Ann's hair, Joe looked at her tear-streaked face and her messed up hair. He murmured, "You're the most beautiful thing I've ever seen in my life."

"Excuse me, sir."

Joe turned. It was the DC-3 pilot with a package in his hand.

"Colonel Crole sent this. Ordered me that upon landing you were to be escorted to the BOQ to get a shower and put on this clean uniform. He told me to tell you that he'd made reservations for the two of you at some pub that has booths where you can talk privately. He said something about it's a good thing to return to the scene of the crime."

Ann looked at Joe. "I don't think I could have made it without Crole."

"Me either."

Later on in the booth in the pub, Joe was contrite. "I am so sorry. I didn't show faith in you. I agonized about it all the time I was escaping from France."

"Oh, no, Joe. I'm the one that should be so sorry. I took you for granted. I don't think any man, particularly someone who is under the stress of combat fatigue, could see the woman he loved so preoccupied with telling another man how much she loved him and not react as you did. And when I got your message that you needed to talk to me and realized how I had taken you for granted, I decided my conduct was unforgivable."

"You mean neither one of us is perfect?"

"Are you just finding out?"

"Round two and we've come through this one without the Brigadier's help."

Chapter XXIII
Engagement

The visits with Ann were glorious. He could drop in at Duxford, borrow a jeep, and get into Cambridge promptly. The professors were kind enough to let him sit in the back of the room during her classes. Joe found history fascinating. He decided, if he got out of this war alive, he was going back for an advanced degree in history.

As they strolled through the campus, Joe asked, "What do you think was Queen Victoria's greatest accomplishment?"

"Her value system."

"Why?"

"It was really a farce with most of the British nobility. But it established a value system that motivated and gave discipline by conscience a great boost. In the United States, particularly rural areas and the West, it became the guiding light."

"You are so right. I grew up in it. You know, you're not only a real scholar, but you have a sense of strategy. Will you marry me?"

Ann gasped, "What!"

"It just popped out. I was so wowed by your mind that I spoke without meaning to."

"Did you mean it?"

"Yes. I've been pondering about how to ask you, and now I messed it up."

"No, you didn't. You spoke from the heart with admiration, and you were comfortable with me. It was wonderful."

"Don't keep me in suspense."

"Of course, I will. I think we had really decided a long time ago. You know you should talk to my parents before we say anything. You don't have to tell them you've already asked me. I suspect they have already figured it out."

"I'll do that, but I don't know when I'll get a chance."

#

The chance came quicker than Joe expected. He had orders to report to General Doolittle to discuss ground forces support with him. He didn't know quite how to prepare for this. He read what he could read, but there wasn't much.

He was ushered into Doolittle's office. "Pleasure to meet you. I like your record."

"Thank you, sir."

"The reason I wanted to talk to you is I want to know what you think. You've had some experience in the South Pacific and you've had experience here. The invasion is coming soon, and the whole issue of tactical air support is going to be important. A number of people are advising me that our heavy bombers can do it. Do you think they can?"

Joe had not thought about this question and he felt anxiety. The surprise was obvious to Doolittle, but he wasn't disappointed.

"Sir, I'm not comfortable with that. Those are high-altitude bombers. Tactical support has to be close to be much good. If those bombers got off target, it would be bad business for our people on the ground."

"I've heard that before. On the other hand, we can dump tons of stuff on the enemy, a lot more than fighters can carry."

"Can't argue with that, sir. When you know it's the enemy, that's great, but I think the risk of hitting our own people is too high. Fighters can do the close support with less risk."

"I understand you engineered something like that in the South Pacific."

"It worked for awhile; that was on Zeros. We couldn't match them in the air. We had to figure what time they'd be taking off, slip in low, and get them before they took off."

"They tell me that you figured that idea out before the rest did. They let you do it because it was your idea and you volunteered for the mission."

"Well, yes, sir, but somebody else would have figured it out anyhow."

Doolittle smiled. "Thank you, Colonel. I appreciate your comments. We're working on some things. If you don't mind, I'll have some people give you a ring from time to time, maybe want you to come down here. While you're here, give yourself another day or so. You squadron commanders work too hard. You must have some time off. There's a lot of war ahead of us yet, and we need our good men."

"Thank you, sir." Joe saluted, walked out the door, and ran smack into Armentrout. They exchanged salutes, dropped fingers; eyebrows up and down the hall went up. Nobody said anything; after all, it was a bird colonel and a brigadier general. They went into an office and had five minutes of exchange.

Armentrout was curious. "How'd it go with the General?"

"I haven't any idea. He asked me about heavies with tactical support, and I said I was scared of it."

"Good for you. You're dead-on with that. I hope you have a little time off before you have to go back."

"Yeah, General told me to take a couple of days. I appreciate that. He said we squadron commanders work too hard."

"He had it right. Four or five of them cracked up and eight or ten went stale. We have to take care of the ones we have left."

"Got something I want to do."

Armentrout grinned. "It wouldn't be what I'm thinkin' you want to do? You're not shopping for a ring, are you?"

"I can't lie to my old C.O. I hope it comes to that. First, I want to talk to her folks."

"Good luck, Joe."

Again they exchanged salutes, again fingers dropped, again the two men parted grinning.

Joe got to a phone and made an appointment to talk with Ann's parents. He felt something he hadn't felt before — fear, flat-out, abject fear. He'd been scared in combat, but he was used to that. He never was terrorized but wasn't sure he didn't feel terror right now. Funny, he hadn't felt that when he'd asked Ann. He was comfortable with Ann. Now he could blow the whole thing. Somehow, he wasn't quite as scared of her mother as he was the old man; that man is a sub-cabinet member. Joe tried to get it together. He dressed in the best he had.

They'd invited him to dinner. That made it scarier. He hoped his table manners were good enough. Again he was grateful to his mother. She thought farmers were somewhat looked down on as being bumpkins. She was fussy about table manners. She told him, if in doubt, work from the outside in with your silverware.

The flat was nice, not spacious, but nice. It showed quality but was not ostentatious. The portions were small because of rationing. He felt guilty using some of their rations.

The conversation was intellectual when they talked about the war. They were cautious not to ask questions about anything that might be secret. They were interested in his background on the farm. As he talked about the farm and his family, Uncle Ed, and Aunt Eve, they were very attentive. They asked questions. They were fascinated with his experience with the sick animals and his going into business with Uncle Ed.

Mr. Bradford commented, "It took a lot of grace on the part of your father to let you go at that early age, particularly when he needed you so badly. Have things gone better on the farm?"

"Oh, yes, they're better. The war in Europe made a big increase in prices. Dad's out of debt now. I don't think Uncle Ed really was that much in debt. Our partnership farm is out of debt. We were able to buy tractors and that greatly increases what we can do. Uncle Ed can work in the fields with his bad leg. They're working awfully hard with the war on. They do their repair work and maintenance at night, so they can use every hour of daylight. Sometimes, they're able to get kids after school to drive the tractors and give Uncle Ed and Dad a chance to work the livestock. Things are going extremely well.

"My pay as a colonel is fairly substantial. I send a good bit of it back to invest in the farm. We certainly aren't wealthy, but we're no longer impoverished. Actually, I think we're all grateful for the experience of going through the Depression and learning what we can do without. It's a good thing to know that you can take care of yourself no matter what. I believe it develops in all of us a creativity that we wouldn't have otherwise."

Joe sensed a growing comfort with Ann's parents. He decided it was time to get to the point. He looked at them, paused, saw her mother's disarming smile, and felt genuine warmth from her father.

"You know, I've been in combat a lot and I've been scared, but I've never been as frightened as I was when I thought about coming down to talk to you people about what I want to talk to you about. Thank you for your kindness. I'm no longer frightened. The reason I'm here is, with great humility, I would like the honor of marrying your daughter."

There was no feigning of surprise, both smiled. Her father answered, "We've been expecting this visit. I think Ann's mother has really been hoping for it. I suppose, like any father with only one daughter, I have been dreading it no matter whom it came from. However, the most important thing on this earth to us is the happiness and well-being of our children. And it's our belief that the happiness of our daughter would greatly diminish if we were to say no. Therefore, you have our blessing."

Joe's obvious relief brought chuckling from both of her parents. Her father looked him in the eye. "Congratulations. I know I'm a biased old man, but I think she's the best there is."

Joe grinned. "That makes two of us. Do you know any place where I can buy a ring? It's hard to buy things, but there must be someplace where people sell fine jewelry when they need to. I'd like to buy her a diamond, not gaudy but excellent quality. Since my mother isn't here to go with me, if you could spare some time to help me, Mrs. Bradford, I would appreciate it."

Mrs. Bradford smiled broadly. "I'd love to."

Her father thought a minute. "Some of my friends in the banks might know of something like this. I'll make a few inquiries in the morning. If you're going to be here during the day, give me a phone number where I can reach you. I'll let you know if I get any decent leads."

"Thank you, sir."

The next afternoon, Joe found himself in the company of Ann's mother in one of the banks looking at an unrolled roll of velvet with several beautiful rings that were part of an estate the bank was liquidating. Much to his amazement, her mother took out a little black object with lenses in it and stuck it in front of her eye. Joe was curious. "What's that?"

"This is a loupe. It gives you a good look. As soon as I'm through, you may have a turn."

He put it to his eye and examined each ring very carefully. You could see if there were blemishes. There was one ring with a caret and a half diamond in the center and two diamonds on each side that caught his eye. He didn't say anything, but he looked at her mother. "Which one do you like?"

She pointed to three, one much smaller and obviously less expensive and two larger ones, one of which was the one that had caught Joe's eye. Joe recognized his future mother-in-law's diplomacy in putting an inexpensive one in the group.

"I think Ann would like any of these."

He asked the price and found that the smaller one was only about 200 pounds, which was $800 and some dollars. The other ones were 700 and 800 pounds. The one he liked best was the most expensive. Spending over $3000 for a ring when ten years before he had been destitute seemed unreasonable, but it was his only chance and he couldn't settle for less. He pointed to the one he liked. "That's my choice. What do you think?"

Her mother smiled with the same radiance he had seen in Ann's smile. "I think that would be lovely."

Joe smiled back. "I want it to be nice. She's going to have to wear it a long time because we don't want to get married until this war is over. And if I get killed, then she'll have something nice that she can keep or sell when she decides to marry someone else."

"Oh, Joe, you're such a pessimist."

"Nah, I'm just pragmatic."

"I'm beginning to understand why Ann loves you. She loves honesty. Sometimes, she's so honest I think it causes her pain when it doesn't need to. I think you're the same way. The two of you ought to get along smashingly."

Chapter XXIV
General Staff

It was mid-afternoon when Ann ran downstairs to answer the telephone. She hurried hoping that it was Joe. It turned out to be her mother.

"Ann, we need you to come down this week-end. Can you do it?"

"I can do it if I don't hear from Joe. He hasn't said anything yet, so I doubt if he'll be calling. Why, what's the matter?"

"We have been asked to entertain a Brigadier General who has been assigned to Eisenhower's staff, some kind of coordinating job. It's awkward just having your father and me. Since we're supposed to make sure that he is well entertained, we'll be going to the theatre, out to dinner, and who knows what else. We just have him for Friday night, Saturday, and Sunday until noon. It would be so nice if you could be with us."

"But, Mother, I'm engaged to Joe. It wouldn't be right for me to be out with somebody else."

"You wouldn't be out with him. We'd be with you the whole time. Everybody would simply expect he was an old friend of the family. We need you, we really do. We don't bother you with many things, but we need you to do this. Your father insists."

"But, Mum, I don't want to."

"I understand that. We know that you love Joe. We know that you're engaged."

"But, Mum, you've always been so proper. This isn't the kind of thing you approve of."

"There's a war on. We wouldn't ask you to do anything improper. Are you going to do it or not? Your father insists."

"Well, if Father insists, I'll have to do it. I'll write Joe today and let him know, so if he hears it from somebody else, he won't be shocked. I don't like this a bit, but I'll do it."

"Good. We'll look for you Friday afternoon."

#

When Ann arrived at her parents' apartment, she felt sick when she saw the overcoat of an American officer with stars on the shoulders hanging in the closet. She walked into the living room and saw her mother. "Mother, I don't like this at all. This just doesn't seem right for Joe."

Her mother looked her straight in the eye with a deadpan expression. "Joe will certainly approve of this. Do not worry about Joe. Your father has insisted. We appreciate you respecting his wishes. You just forget about all these things that are worrying you, come in the other room, and meet the General."

With great annoyance and almost rebellion, she thought about grabbing her coat and leaving because she couldn't understand her mother, she couldn't understand her father, and she disliked the whole situation. However, they had never ever betrayed her. She belligerently walked into the room planning to let that general know that she was going to keep her distance.

Her mother walked ahead of her. "General, I'd like to have you meet our daughter, Ann."

The General turned around and looked at Ann. Ann's hostility froze and she screamed, "Joe!"

Her mother, her father, and Joe all burst out laughing, as she planted a passionate kiss on his lips and hugged him with intensity. Her father reached over and kissed her mother.

"Joe, what happened?"

"I'm not quite sure what happened. Somehow, this position came up. I think my predecessor's plane went down, and they needed someone to work in liaison between Eisenhower's staff and the Air Corps staff and the whole issue of planning ground support. Apparently, several people recommended me and I was ordered down here. You probably wondered where I was and why I hadn't called. I haven't had a minute. They told me not to tell anybody, at first. I suspect we're paranoid about secrecy. After cramming instructions for three or four days, they told me to take some time off, so I got in touch with your folks and we made up this little conspiracy."

"What a wonderful conspiracy. You people are my everything."

#

Early the following Monday morning, Eighth Air Force chief of staff received the salute of a young brigadier general and heard, "Brigadier General Joe Oberlin reporting as ordered, sir."

"Sit down, Joe. We have a lot to do, and we have to do it fast."

"Yes, sir."

"You seem a little uncomfortable. What's the problem?"

"Well, sir, I don't believe I deserve to be here."

"You wouldn't be here if you didn't deserve it. I understand you've used all of your spare time to read all the West Point textbooks on military strategy and tactics, that you have an excellent record both as a pilot, a flight commander, and as a squadron commander. I understand you fought in both the Pacific and the European theater and that you understand fighter aircraft as well as anybody we have."

"Thank you, sir. I doubt that's accurate, but thank you."

"Armentrout would have wanted you to have this job."

Joe gasped, "Would have? What are you talking about?"

"He went down."

"Went down? Where? How?"

"You know Armentrout. He wanted to know all about everything. He said he couldn't evaluate strategic bombers and their tactical utility if he hadn't been flying in them. Flew deadhead on a raid into Germany and those lucky Krauts got his plane. No reports of any parachutes. They went into a cloudbank. There is still some hope but no reports of survivors. He's out of it. He talked about you to a lot of people. That's what made us look into your record. Everybody's sure that Armentrout would have picked you."

"But, sir, he was a West Pointer. There are other West Pointers around who could have been picked."

"Yes, sir, there are and they're good, too. But you have something we wanted."

"What's that, sir?"

"Every team you work with gets a "We" spirit. Don't know where it comes from. Some people make fun of you, but none of them make fun of you as a combat officer."

"Thank you, sir."

"Let's get to business. You're here, it's your duty to do your job, now forget all that other crap."

"Yes, sir."

"Our problem is we have to keep losses to a minimum, and we have to do everything we can with air support. Some of those ground officers don't know up from sic cum about what airplanes can do and what they can't do. They're going to make unreasonable, sometimes ridiculous demands. On the other hand, we have a lot of sky jockeys over here who think they know everything about close ground support and most of them don't. This situation has a potential to kill a lot of our own people. It's your job to help keep losses to a minimum and work out the system where we can understand each other. I hope to God that you can get the ear of Ike's staff. That's why we put the star on this position. Figured it had to be a general or they wouldn't pay any attention.

"Now, so much for the orders. You want a bit of advice?"

"Yes, sir."

"I hear you're pretty religious. That's all right, that's your business. The people you work with, if they have any brains, will respect you for it, but there are a lot of them who will think you're some sort of a nut. Why don't you tone it down and only talk about it when they ask you."

"Yes, sir. Thank you for the advice. Anything else, sir?"

"No, you have an appointment with Bedell Smith at 1300 hours. He's one of the best, and he has Ike's ear. You can trust him."

"Thank you, sir."

Knowing Bedell Smith by reputation, Joe arrived ten minutes early.

At 1300 hours sharp, an orderly appeared. "General Oberlin, the General will see you now."

"Have a seat, Joe."

Joe sat down, uncomfortably. Somehow, in the presence of this sharp mind, Joe felt more anxiety than he did when he saw Messerschmidts or Zeros in the distance.

Bedell Smith looked him in the eye. "You're very young, but you're highly recommended. You know what we're up against."

"Yes, sir. I understand the assignment, but it's not going to be easy."

"None of this is easy. Of course, it's tough. You're put there because you can handle tough assignments."

"Yes, sir."

"How do you plan to approach it?"

"Sir, it seems to me the first thing I better do is talk to front-line, combat-experienced officers and see what they need."

A flick of a smile appeared at the corner of Bedell's mouth. "Good thinking. What do you want from this office?"

"Nothing, sir, except if things get real sticky, we may need a referee."

"That's what I'm here for. Anything else?"

"No, sir."

"One more thing, Ike wants to meet you."

"Ike?"

"Yes, sir. He likes to meet all the new officers around here. You'll like him."

"Yes, sir."

"Be there at 1400."

"Yes, sir."

Joe saluted and left. Bedell was to the point, tough, and smart. He was satisfied that Joe was on the right track. When he needed him, Bedell would be there.

Ten minutes before 1400 hours, Joe was waiting in the outer office of the Supreme Commander. About 1355 hours, the orderly picked up a paper with a list on it and went in. At two minutes before 1400, Joe followed his escort into General Eisenhower's office. As he saluted, he was amazed. It was like meeting Uncle Ed. Eisenhower's grin made him feel relaxed.

Ike looked Joe in the eye. "Sit down, Joe, just wanted to take a little time to get acquainted. Read a brief on you. You're young to be where you are. Do you think you can handle it?"

"Honestly, sir, I don't know. I'll give it the very best I have. I hope that's enough."

Ike smiled. "You'll do all right. You'd worry me if you were too sure of yourself. I understand that you have some shyness about wearing medals."

"Yes, sir."

"What's the problem? What bothers you?"

"I don't think I'm a hero, sir. The real heroes are dead."

Ike was thoughtful. "Joe, you and I have something in common. When I read in the papers how 'Eisenhower Won in North Africa', I thought of all those dead people at Kasserine Pass and elsewhere. They're the heroes, they and the men who slugged through sandstorms. They took the casualties and they won the battles. When I see the headlines, *'Eisenhower Wins in Sicily'* it makes me uncomfortable. Nevertheless, we have to win a war, and there are some things we can't change.

"Nice meeting you, Joe. Glad to have you aboard."

"Thank you, sir." Joe saluted and left.

Chapter XXV
Ground Combat

Joe was sitting in the radio compartment of a B-17 hopping from Britain, to Gibraltar, to Italy where he planned to see ground fighting first hand. He had time to think and ruminate. Shortly, he began to chuckle. The other deadheaders looked at him wondering what on earth could make this man in this noisy, rattling B-17 laugh. He didn't bother to explain. He was thinking about Crole. Crole was now the C.O. of his old squadron. It amused him that Crole was now in the position of enforcing all of the disciplines for which he had held so much internal contempt.

He wondered how many subordinates would say Crole and then stick a sir on it to avoid insubordination the way Crole had done to Armentrout. He wondered how he'd crack down on the hotshots, how trim that squadron was going to be. Crole had grown up. He understood that discipline saves lives. He'd given up antics like flying upside-down in a formation. Few would remember them. He'd do all right. He sure knew flying. Crole always said he was a better pilot than Joe was, but Joe was a better shot than he was. He was right. Crole now had downed seventeen enemy planes compared to Joe's eleven. Crole was impatient, but he'd do well in the job. What a marvelous friend, so different, so little in common. Only a war would throw them together. He'd be a friend till death. The other passengers looked over and observed the young brigadier general doze off to sleep, smiling.

#

Two days later, as artillery shells were bursting around the command post of Infantry Captain Gunman, an orderly from headquarters came crawling up followed by a stranger. Gunman snapped, "What in the hell do you want?"

"Orders from headquarters, sir. Had to bring this general up here."

"What in the . . . Why are you here?"

"Captain, I have some responsibility for coordinating air support with the ground troops. To do it right, I need to see how it really is, so I asked to see a company commander in the thick of it. They sent me up to you. I'll try not to get in the way. Tell me what I ought to know. I've been told you're a good officer."

Gunman observed the terrain and then he snapped, "Keep your head down. They have snipers out there."

Gunman looked like a combat officer ought to look; he needed a shave, probably smelled bad if you got close to him. He showed dirt streaks, a bullet hole in the shoulder of his jacket, a dent in his metal helmet, and four days of beard.

Joe spoke up. "Gunman, when you have time, I'd appreciate knowing what's going on and what the Air Corps could do to help."

Gunman frowned. "Up here, we don't have much time to talk or think. Sometimes things get screwed up and we get hit by friendly fire. Those are the worst casualties. Sending the boys back with their guts in a pile on the stretcher is bad any time, but when it's from our own fire, it's awful."

"If the Air Corps tried to work more closely, what would happen?"

"Be worse. I watched them hit Monte Cassino. They hit it some, but they plowed the fields around it. Bombers are too clumsy for ground support."

"That's why I'm here, to learn."

Just then, there was a whine from a shell. Gunman and his orderly dove into a trench. Joe, sensing they knew what they were doing, dove in behind them. The shell burst blowing up dirt and debris. The captain and his orderly were brushing themselves off as Joe got up shaking like a dog coming out of the water.

Gunman looked over and laughed. "General, you're looking like a fighting man now. You were a little slow on the dive. You better be quicker next time."

Joe had a mouthful of dirt and was coughing from the dust. He croaked, "What can the Air Corps do to help you?"

"Knock the Krauts out of the air and beat them up behind the lines and at home."

"Care if I hang around awhile? Seem to be learning more here than I can any place else."

"Choose your poison, man. You're welcome. Kind of pleasant to have somebody from headquarters interested in what we're doing."

Joe spent three days with Gunman. Then he flew a couple missions with the heavy bombers.

#

Joe had just returned when the General sent word he wanted to see him immediately.

The General glared at Joe. "We don't promote people to general to have them spend three days in the trenches and take flights on bombers. We lost Armentrout that way. We don't want to lose you. What do you think you're doing?"

"Sir, you have to know the facts before you can make the decisions. The way to know the facts is to see what's going on yourself. Anyway, sir, they told me they had two or three West Pointers who could handle this job if anything happened to me."

The General grinned. "You're a bit unconventional, but that's what makes the American soldier what he is. I hope you understand it was my duty to chew you out."

"Yes, sir."

"What are your thoughts now?"

"Sir, they're not my thoughts, they're the thoughts of the best people I could find. They think heavy bombers are too crude. There's going to be a lot of pressure to use heavies because they can plow the countryside, but they aren't precise enough.

The Air Corps' job is to control the air, destroy the enemy's ability to produce, keep enemy supplies and reinforcements from getting to the front, and provide tactical-fighter ground support. A young captain with a lot of moxie down in Italy told me every helmet and every vehicle ought to have good markings, otherwise, when they break out, they're going to get blown up by our own airplanes."

"Write up your report, and then I'd like to have you review some other things before they go on."

Joe looked with alarm. "Sir, are you gonna make a desk jockey out of me?"

"I don't think we could, but even a good racehorse spends some time in the stall. You're going to serve your hitch."

"Yes, sir."

Joe found himself reviewing plans. He was grateful for his father's teaching when he was young. You looked over the flock of sheep for the first little nuance of illness so that you could isolate and treat them before it became epidemic in the flock. That was what he was doing now, looking for the little nuances that might lead to bigger trouble later on. Joe couldn't get them all, but he did what he could.

The fringe benefit of the current assignment was he had regular hours. For the first time, he could live an organized life. He spent a great deal of time with Ann's parents. Ann was able to come to London every weekend and occasionally during the week.

The Bradfords were jokers like the Oberlins. When he showed them a copy of the picture of his little sister Annie poking a finger on his nose, they hooted with laughter saying, "You Yanks are raucous. Don't know if that would get much approval in Britain, but it should. We can hardly wait to meet that little sister."

"She's not really little any more. She's twenty-one now. You will like her. She's a ray of sunshine in any room."

"You talk about growing up in poverty. You really grew up in wealth."

"I know. I'm glad you can see it."

Sometimes, the Brigadier came to town, too. He had changed greatly. Apparently, his financial stress and his suspicions of Barkley had bothered him more than he knew.

He had finally decided that World War II was a real war and could be, at least in some ways, compared to the Great War. Ever since the Brigadier had unlimbered and shown Joe and Ann his scars, he seemed to be more light-hearted. He was amusing in London because he never lost the aura of the Brigadier in terms of commands to cab drivers, an occasional bobby on the street, or anyone who he was paying to do anything.

Chapter XXVI
Crole

Joe, Ann, and her parents went up to visit at Bradford Hall and Joe paid a surprise visit to his old squadron. When he walked in to Crole's office, he found him with his feet on the desk, a newspaper over his face, sound asleep beside an ashtray full of cigarette butts. Instead of waking him, Joe decided to look things over. He saw many friendly faces and had short, happy reunions, but what he noticed most was the base was sharp, the planes were sharp, the salutes were sharp, and the uniforms were clean and neatly pressed. There was no grease or oil to speak of around the planes or on the runways. The grounds and barracks were neat. There was no litter. "Holy Smoke! Has Crole become a martinet?" The picture of Crole sound asleep with the newspaper over his face crossed Joe's mind.

He returned to headquarters, walked in, and yelled in a loud voice, "Out of the sack!"

The newspaper flew. Crole jumped. He looked at Joe with his lip curling down but the sides of his mouth turned up. "Oberlin, sir, what are you trying to do? I'm the C.O. of this squadron, and I can sleep if I want to." Grinning widely, Crole jumped up, reached out, and shook Joe's hand. "It's just great to see you."

Much to his amazement, Joe saw an immaculately clean uniform. Crole was cleanly shaven, fingernails well manicured and clean, and he looked sharp. The complete opposite of what he expected to see come out from under the newspaper. "You're really looking G.I., Crole. What has come over you?"

"This is our outfit and the 'We' spirit has finally overcome me. Some people say I'm working too many hours, but they don't know how many catnaps I get in the office. Only my orderly knows that. That's what keeps me going, that and cigarettes and some booze from time to time."

"Who carries you home now?"

"Don't have to now, too much responsibility. Take only a little now and then and only when we're grounded."

They sat for a minute and just looked at each other, grinning. Joe was first to speak. "Wish I were back flying. I only get an occasional hop now. I miss it."

"I betcha do. It would be a sentence to me to do what you have to do even if they gave me a star for it."

"You look good under those chickens. You're doing what you want to do which is pretty much what you always did anyhow. I'm glad you overcame the extreme renegade in you. It hid your talent, but I hope you didn't get rid of all of it. I enjoyed it."

"Don't worry about that. I can never lose all of it. When you getting married?"

"After the war."

"That poor girl is a paragon of patience. You better be careful, she'll get tired of waiting and find somebody who isn't as stubborn as you are."

"She's just as stubborn as I am. If I were insisting, she'd want to wait, but the way it is, she can blame me for it, and it makes everybody happy."

"I think you're probably full of it, but if that makes you feel good go ahead.

"The Brigadier didn't lose his affection for the base after you left. He is our semi-official inspector, walking around, coming in and telling me what he likes and what he doesn't like. He is really quite helpful. The men all like him, enlisted men in particular. He has that stiff backbone and choppy way of talking. They like to ask him questions, so they can hear his answer. They particularly like to ask him about The War and the Great War. He isn't above spinning a few yarns with crew chiefs when they are waiting on their planes to come back. It is good for him, good for them, and it helps me. He makes worthwhile suggestions. Some of the men have a hard time keeping a straight face when he gives his British salute. I'm even learning how to play chess."

"What are you going to do after the war, Crole?"

"Oh, I'm goin' back to school, get an advanced degree, get a real good job, get married, and have a whole bunch of kids. Teach them all how to fly upside-down and how to ward off the influence of squares like you. What are you gonna do?"

"I'm going to get married right away and then I think I'll go back to school. I've enjoyed reading military history, and I think I'd like to study history more in general. Won't ever give up the farm as long as Uncle Ed and Dad can farm it. They don't need me anyhow. Annie's getting pretty interested in a man who wants to farm. I'd like to get advanced degrees and Ann would like to, too. Maybe we can find someplace where we could both teach and raise a family."

"You're not going to stay in the army since you got your star?"

"I don't think so. Our country has a history of gutting the military after a war. A rookie one-star sure isn't going to last. I think I'll stay in the reserves. I like that idea. I could fly on the weekends and keep up with the new stuff when it comes along.

"I have to go now. I just couldn't resist stopping by." Joe looked straight at Crole. "Take care of yourself, Crole. You and I have both burned up more luck than any two people are entitled to. It would go hard with me if anything happened to you."

Crole grinned. "You desk jockeys all worry about us who fly. You take care of yourself, too. Unless I miss my guess, you'll find some way to get in the action when you can."

"Thanks, Crole. Bye." A friendly cork to the shoulder was followed by one from Crole. They exchanged salutes and Joe left.

Joe mused to himself; we never want to think we're good. Somebody goes ahead and starts a squadron and you come along and make it better. If you're not careful, you think you're important. You leave and somebody else comes along and makes it better yet. We're all links in a chain.

That afternoon, Joe, Ann, and her family were sitting on a side porch of Bradford Hall when a young man brought in a flock of sheep. Joe's face lit up. "Ann, do you want a lesson about life?"

Ann looked at him quizzically, her parents looked at him with surprise, and the Brigadier merely moved his eyes sideways and asked, "What are you talking about, General?"

"Come out to the barn and I'll show you."

Ann reluctantly agreed. Then he looked at her parents and the Brigadier. "You can come, too, if you want to."

Shortly thereafter, Joe put a low pole between the two lots and told the young man chasing the sheep to crowd them and make them jump over the pole. The first sheep jumped over the pole. Joe promptly pulled the pole away and the entire flock jumped over the spot where the pole had been without ever looking. Joe looked up. "How's that for a lesson?"

Ann and her family looked quizzical, not understanding. Joe asked, "You mean you don't get it?"

They shook their heads.

"Well, sheep are stupid. Sheep are the dumbest critters you ever have to deal with. One of the great revelations of my life was when, as a small child, I first heard the talk about the Lord being my shepherd. It really made sense to me. My father was a real shepherd. He was so smart and the sheep were so dumb. If the Lord is our shepherd, His wisdom is infinite. We are His sheep and compared to Him we are stupid. If God has infinite wisdom, which we as mere mortals can't comprehend, it stands to reason that he deserves our worship.

The first to speak was the Brigadier. "By Jove, a religious lesson out of a bunch of sheep. Good boy there, good man, good man."

Ann's parents smiled. Her father was thoughtful. "You're a philosopher, Joe, hadn't seen that side of you before."

Ann was indignant. "I see it all the time. This man knows animals and he learns from them."

That evening, in the compartment on the train on the way back to London, they were very tired, leaning back, and dozing. Joe, with drowsy eyelids, looked over at Ann's father to see him saying something over and over. Joe leaned forward to listen.

"Stupid sheep, wise shepherds. Stupid humans, Infinite God. That barnyard theology beats what I get in the cathedrals. Don't ever want to forget that one." Joe smiled and dozed off.

#

Just three weeks later, Joe was sitting at his desk and the phone rang. It was Haman, flight commander of B Flight.

"General Oberlin?"

"Yes, sir."

"This is Haman, B Flight."

"Hi, Haman, how are you? Good to hear from you."

"Not good to hear from me. Crole bought it today."

"What!"

"He's dead."

"What!"

"We were flying escort on some B-17s on a raid near Berlin. Three Faulkwolf 190s came out of the sun. Somehow, they must have identified Crole as the boss pilot because all three came down on him. They simply ganged him — one in the center and one on each side — and they shot him up some. His plane was damaged, but he out flew them and got away. Then one of those new Kraut jets, a ME262, caught him. They're at least a hundred miles an hour faster than the P51. He didn't have a chance. There was a blinding, bright yellow flash, and his plane spiraled down and hit the ground. I followed him down, no chute. I saw him hit the ground. No hope on this one. Sorry, sir, but I thought you'd want to know right away."

"Thank you, Haman. We lost a great one."

"Yes, sir, we did."

"Thanks again, bye."

Joe hung up and felt his skin tighten up all over his face. He stood up and took a deep breath. It felt like his heart was sinking into his churning stomach. He sat down with a crash, as visions of Crole's puckish grin came over him. He thought of the great yellow flash and the downward spiral. His pain intensified, as he muttered, "And I wasn't there."

Ten minutes later, Bedell Smith stuck his head in Joe's office. "Did you get those reports on..." and stopped mid-sentence. "Good God, Joe. What's the matter? You're as white as a sheet."

Joe looked up, hands limp, and slack jawed. "Crole bought it today. Best pilot I knew. We got our wings together clear back in early '42. He was a Triple Ace, but more than that, he turned into a real leader. We lost a great one, and I lost my best friend. He always ridiculed me, always made fun of me, but I always knew that in any kind of a fight he'd be there just like I would be for him. He bought it and I wasn't there." Joe choked and wept.

The usually curt Bedell showed genuine sympathy. Joe regained his voice. "You know, I was a lousy athlete. They said I walked like a clodhopper and bounced like a cork. I couldn't run. Crole coached me. He was a great athlete. He coached me till I beat him." Joe smiled faintly. "Never forget the day I beat him. He didn't know whether to be furious or proud of himself."

Bedell smiled, stayed a few minutes, listened, and then spoke softly. "Sorry, Joe, I know how it is. These things can wait. Take the afternoon off. Give Ann a call. Give yourself some slack. You'll need it. We all need it from time to time."

"Thank you, sir."

Joe went to his flat and called Ann, who gasped and sobbed softly, as he was talking.

"Oh, Joe, I hurt so much, but most of all I hurt for you. I know what he meant to you and what you meant to him. Take some satisfaction in what you meant to him."

After he hung up, Joe thought about calling Maggie McQuire, so she could tell the nurses. Half of those nurses probably still had hopes of landing Crole. But he didn't call. Maggie's network was better than anybody's. She already knew, probably knew before he did.

Then he sat down to write Crole's parents. He finished one line: *On this day, the American Army lost a truly great officer* — at which point, he put down his pen, put on his trench coat and cap, and took a long walk in the rain.

Chapter XXVII
Perception

In the weeks that followed Crole's death, Joe took many lonely walks, often in the rain, sometimes with Ann who had learned Joe's love of walking even in the rain.

"Ann, it's all wrong."

"What's all wrong?"

"What we're doing."

"Doing what?"

"This war."

"Don't you think we have to stop Hitler? Haven't you heard about his death camps?"

"Of course, we have to stop Hitler, but the whole thing is all wrong."

"Are you upset about Crole?"

"Yes, but it's a lot more than that."

"Like what?"

"Every day we put a thousand plane raids over Germany destroying factories and a lot of other things. We kill a lot of innocent people who may not like Hitler. Then at night, the RAF plows up their cities killing innocent people like children who are too little to know who Hitler is."

Ann looked at Joe. Gentle raindrops had collected on her face as she spoke. "If we don't stop Hitler, more will die."

Joe put up an umbrella and pulled Ann near him. "I know, but we shouldn't have let it come to this. Are we any better off as people than thousands of years ago? The Romans, the Persians, the Crusaders all did horrible things, but they didn't kill people as the world does today. Stalin murdered thousands upon thousands and he is okay just because Hitler is worse. Does that make sense?"

"Only in the short run. But Joe, what is the answer?"

Joe held Ann close as a double-decker bus passed by, and then they crossed over to the park. "The short answer is to win this war and contain the communists afterward. The bigger answer is to stop the Hitlers and Stalins before they get strong, but the real answer is to create good will so the haters can't get strong."

"How do we do that?"

"That's why I want to study history. I want to know if the Romans' Pax Romana really worked. I want to know what makes for greater peace. I want to know if strength makes peace. I want to know if religious faith makes peace. I want to know why Muslims with intense faith are cruel fighters and how Christians with intense faith could have an inquisition or burn witches. It seems to me we need to study a lot more history, or we will make the same mistakes over and over."

"Oh, Joe, you do worry so much and you do think heavy thoughts, but you are searching for the right answers. We can search together, but we must have fun or we won't think wisely."

Ann stopped walking. "Joe, what are you staring at?"

"That kid over there in the soccer game."

Ann looked at the muddy kids playing in the drizzle and asked, "Which one?"

Joe looked at the hodgepodge gathering of kids who had sorted themselves into two teams. "The one the other kids are throwing off their team."

"Why are they doing that?"

"Didn't you see?"

"No."

"He's so slow and clumsy that the ball bounced off his head, went into the net, and scored a goal for the other team."

Joe walked rapidly to the soccer field and put a hand on the shoulder of the moist-eyed, rejected boy. The boy looked up in surprise. "Do I know you?"

"You do now. We are brothers under the skin."

"What does that mean?"

"It means we're alike."

The soccer game stopped, as awestruck boys stared at the wings and ribbons on the tall American officer. One of the older kids yelled out, "He has command-pilot wings."

Both teams gathered around Joe and stared in childish awe.

Joe looked at his new friend. "What's your name?"

"Mike Bradley."

"Have you played much football?"

"Not much. I was sick when I was younger."

"We are brothers under the skin. All this will make you stronger and you'll have a richer life."

One of the older players asked, "Did I hear you say you were Mike's brother?"

"Something like that."

"Mike never told us."

"There is probably a lot you don't know about Mike. If you help him in soccer, he might help you in a lot of other ways."

"Mike is smart."

"And a lot more. He's wise. Did you see how he kept calm when you were mean to him?"

"Yeah."

"You have to have that to be a good leader. He was the only one I could see here who had it.

"Mike, we have to go now. Here's my card with my home address. Stop by and we'll make a time to talk some more."

As they turned to go, he heard a voice say, "We want Mike on our side."

Ann squeezed Joe's hand. "I think that's how it will all start.

Chapter XXVIII
Failure?

A youthful major stuck his head into Joe's office and snapped, "Did you hear about Normandy?"

"What about it?"

"They used heavy bombers for ground support, missed, and killed a bunch of our people."

"Thank you, Major."

Joe picked up the phone. "Get me Ann Bradford."

"Ann, I failed."

"How?"

"They used heavy bombers to support ground troops and killed a bunch of our own people."

"You did your best."

"And I failed. I should have refused the job and let some West Pointer do it. They probably would have listened to him."

"You don't know that."

"I don't, but I do know that I failed."

"Did Churchill fail when he preached preparedness and couldn't move the government?"

"Yes."

"Did he give up?"

"No."

"Are you going to?"

"No."

"Are you a little spoiled because so many things have gone so well for you?"

"I was a flop as a kid. I darn near was court-martialed and I lost Crole. Is that having things go well?"

"You aren't a Jew in Germany."

"You win."

"Pick up some books on the people you admire the most. See how you feel after you read them."

"Okay, but a bunch of people are dead because I failed to convince the top brass."

"Did you do your best?"

"I tried."

"That's all you can do. If you don't stop this, I'll stick the Brigadier on you. He felt the same way more than once during the Great War."

"He did?"

"You didn't think you were unique, did you? Read history."

"Thanks, Ann."

"Joe, do you ever wonder if you are such a worry-wart and self-blamer that you figure wrong and hurt yourself?"

"Ouch! What do you mean?"

"Have you ever thought that maybe you didn't fail, maybe you succeeded?"

"What are you talking about? Good men are dead."

"How many?"

"We don't know yet but over a hundred."

"I've read that a lot more than that have been lost taking some objectives."

"Not from our own planes."

"Pipe down and listen to me. If our army was losing lots more men than that and not able to take an important place, the top brass might decide we might lose fewer men if they destroyed it with bombers. If they did, they would consider your warning, be more careful, and go ahead knowing that even if they killed some of our own men it would be fewer than not doing it."

"Thanks, Ann, you put me in focus. The top brass are good men. They have to make awful decisions."

"I love you and I don't want anyone to hurt my man, even you."

"How I do love you, Ann. Thanks for picking me up."

Joe put down the phone and sighed. "I have to get out from behind this desk."

#

Later, he was able to draw an assignment as a deputy wing commander in France and flew some before the war ended. Then he received orders to return to England to work on logistics of who would go to the Pacific and how they would get them there.

They were still working on this when the A-bomb landed and the war ended.

Chapter XXIX
Marriage

The wedding was held in the Methodist Church in the village. Coming out of the church, there was an arch made of sabers held by a mixture of staff officers from the Supreme Command and pilots from his old squadron. The Brigadier had borrowed the swords and sabers from two museums in order to make an arch that met his specifications.

The wedding came off with military precision; the Brigadier having a strong influence on Ann's parents as well as some thoughts of his own. When they walked out under the arch of sabers, there was a deafening roar, as a formation of P-51s flew over. The last one on the outside was flying upside-down. The thoughtful Haman remembered that was one of Crole's favorite pranks and did it for Joe. A gaunt but happy Armentrout was best man. Armentrout had survived German prison camp and was now sporting two stars on each shoulder.

Bradford Hall was decorated and fairly rocked during the reception.

When Joe and Ann went to the car to leave, there was much throwing of rice and shouting of good wishes. Armentrout escorted them out, closed the door, saluted, and dropped three fingers leaving just one as he looked Joe in the eye. Joe returned the salute — dropped three fingers. The knowing pilots of the squadron all grinned broadly, as the mystified, formal officers from headquarters looked on in bewilderment. The driver sped down the road.

Ann wistfully asked, "Do you think I will fit in, in the States?"

Joe smiled faintly. "How did you put it the night we met? 'You'll be over there; you won't be over paid. The question is…' "

That's as far as he got. Ann's pointer finger poked the end of his nose, as she snapped, "That's far enough!"

Epilogue

As the Osgoods finished their story, Mrs. Osgood was concerned. "I'm afraid we have gone on too long. We old people do that."

Dr. Grace Cannon answered warmly, "Oh, no. You have been a great help. We want this history to show people what made our university what it is."

Mrs. Osgood's eyes sparkled. "Joe was always my hero."

"Many people say 'they' were our university's greatest president. Joe was a good administrator, and Ann was a brilliant scholar who wrote great textbooks and novels. Her lectures with that marvelous, lyrical, British accent were so successful that even the ultimate academicians respected her. Their children did well, too. Crole was a White House fellow, Eve made law review at Harvard, and the younger ones are doing just as well."

She paused, and then continued. "Joe is so humble. When people mention it, he reminds them of what Churchill said about Attlee, 'A humble man who has a lot to be humble about.'

"I think he was no doubt a fine scholar, but the thing that made him a great president is that he always identified with the students who had difficulties and problems — particularly with those who felt rejected."

Annie Oberlin Osgood smiled. "That's our Joe."

About the Book

This is a family-friendly novel, rich in historical detail and engaging characters, like books by James Michener.

Unable to compete in sports, tone deaf, and behind in school as a child, shy Joe Oberlin's social awkwardness also stems from burn scars. As the Depression deepens, he learns he has a gift for unconventional farming and a family that believes in him. Then he learns to fly. A World War II fighter pilot, he sticks to his old-fashioned country values, which clash with those of an urban superior who persecutes him. Supported by his flamboyant friend Crole, in the skies he faces fear and death; on the ground he meets a brilliant British woman to whom his "unconventional conventionality" matters.

About the Author

Raised on a farm in rural Indiana, William W. Erwin was a 20 year-old member of the Army Air Corps in WW2. He bought his first 80 acres with money earned from 4H projects. With a degree in agricultural economics from the University of Illinois, he also fed a passion for history through continuing education classes... and by keeping his latest history read under his bed every night. A life-long farmer and public servant, he served as a state senator, Assistant Secretary of Agriculture, EPA environmental expert, and noted public speaker. A world traveler, he told countless stories to his grandchildren on the backroads of Europe. His gift for storytelling is now available to all in a charming trio of historical fiction books, suitable for children and adults alike.

Erwin is the author of three books:
Angus, Sapling in the Brambles and *Two Clouds*
All three will soon be available at:
http://www.erwinbooks.com
and
http://www.unlimitedpublishing.com/erwin